ASTRO GIRLS

CELESTIAL BOND

ISHA PANESAR

Editor: Dannielle Line
Interior design: Ida Jansson

National Library of Australia Cataloguing-in-Publication data:
Astro Girls/Isha Panesar

ISBN: 978-0-6450180-0-4 (sc)
ISBN: 978-0-6489847-1-9 (e)

"It's a beautiful thing to watch a new author shine. Astro Girls is an inspiring debut novel by author Isha Panesar."
Sarah, Duchess of York

Power awakens your compass
It aids your bearings
It tests your mettle
But if you are weak, evil will follow.

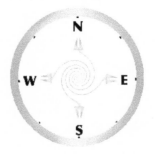

For Bradley, Aiyanna and Lycan

Contents

Acknowledgments

"Your dreams (no matter how big) will forever be dreams, if you don't find the courage and persistence to bring them to life."

I found it, and when I thought about all the special individuals who helped me, so you could now hold this book in your hands. My thoughts, without question, first visit my loving fiancé Bradley, who had always nurtured my dreams, believed in my abilities, and who inspires me that every day is an opportunity to make dreams come true. I have never felt stronger.

To my beautiful, avid reading daughter, Aiyanna, (who surpassed my height by the age of eleven!) when

I'd ponder on the ideas for Astro Girls as a novel, I wanted it to be special to you. You were my flair for writing this. To my little – handsome – Prince Lycan, who fills me with joy every waking moment.

To my 'fairy godmother', who was one of the first souls to read my raw manuscript and believed in my ability to make Astro Girls a success. I thank you immensely, for your unwavering kindness and support. I have always found your generosity enchanting and I am forever grateful to you.

To Karen McDermott – where do I start? I am truly grateful to you, for visioning this novel in your new publishing house. You are another enchanting soul I have met on my author journey, so welcoming, understanding, supportive, calm and humble with the biggest heart. You put me at ease no matter how big or small my (many) worries were, I will always remember what you have done for me, thank you. To your team at White Light Publishing, I thank Dannielle for working with me on the numerous edits, to Dylan, Chelsea and Rachel for helping behind the scenes on this novel.

To my big sister Preety, for planning operation 'free bird'.

THE ENTRY

Chapter 1

My name is Arianna. I'm twelve years old, and I'm a Taurus.

Taurus! That's funny. You see, star signs never used to interest me too much. Until... well, I'm about to tell you.

After several recent life-changing events, I've come straight here to write down every single detail before I forget anything important. You never know, I may need to refer to this in the future.

I think it's best to start way back when all this

began.

About a year ago, my family and I moved here to the beautiful, luscious green borough of Surrey Heath. It was all down to my stepdad. He was about to land his biggest contract deal.

"YES! Baby, it's finally here!" Brad shouted in utter excitement as he rushed back from the hallway.

Yuck! the cutesy nicknames still sent my gagging reflexes into overdrive. It's not so much for the gross word choice, but more because of the babyish tone used.

"What is it?" Mum replied puzzled before taking a sip of her freshly squeezed orange juice.

"The contract!" He replied, as he ripped open the dull white, A4 sized envelope and engrossed himself amongst its endless supply of pages.

"It's a bit early for post. The postmen clearly don't sleep much around here. Baby, why don't you sit down and eat your breakfast first, before it gets cold?" Mum suggested.

There was no reply; as though my stepdad had been paused in real time. The only thing in motion were his denim blue eyes shifting back and forth like a typewriter carriage would have.

[Sigh] "How are you feeling about your first day, Arianna? Is your school bag all packed?"

"Yes, I packed it all last night. I'm fine, Mum."

I wasn't fine, not at all. In fact, I was so petrified

I'd mindlessly stirred my porridge until it turned into a cold, watery slop. I mean, I wasn't just moving into a new school; I was starting my first year in a private school. Which I only got into because my parents thought they'd try their luck and to our surprise, I was accepted. Urgh! What if I stuck out like a sore thumb? This is why I don't want to make a big deal about it. I want to hold some sense of numbness on the topic; it helped with the tension.

"Ok, well when you've finished your breakfast, I'll take you."

"Oh, I thought Brad was taking me?"

"Ha, look at him! I don't think your stepdad is going to move from that spot all day, let alone take you to school. It's fine, I'll take you, finish up."

Great! I was kind of looking forward to the drive into school with Brad, at least. He has a knack for making me feel at ease, plus he doesn't keep probing me with questions like Mum does. Maybe that's because he wouldn't feel comfortable, you know, not being my biological dad and all.

I scrapped the slop from my bowl down into the sink, made my way through the hallway and grabbed my schoolbag on the way out. It was the usual wet, glum weather you'd expect here in England and most definitely at this time of year. It was belting down with rain and Mum had already warmed up the car. I made a clear run for it, quickly soldiering on through the rain until I got to the passenger's side. I yanked hard on the handle and slammed the door shut behind my soaking wet shoes. Mum sat there, idle for a moment with both of her hands grabbing the steering wheel firmly. She stared ahead out of the empty driveway.

"Mum?" I called, trying to nudge her from her daydream.

My voice didn't startle her at all. She took a deep breath and sighed outwardly.

"Is your seatbelt on?" she replied in a monotone voice, resuming her blank gaze.

"Yes, Mum. You honestly don't have to do this; I know it's hard for you," I empathised.

"It's fine, Arianna."

And that's exactly where I get it from, the 'shrugging it off' when something is a big deal. Three months ago, Mum had a traumatic experience while driving. She'd hit a deer. It came out of nowhere and the damage 'wrote off' her car. Luckily, she was OK and my younger brother Lycan and I weren't in the car. She hadn't gotten over it. In fact, she hasn't driven since. So, you can imagine my shock that today (of all days) she bravely gets back behind the wheel. I knew it wouldn't be the atmosphere to ease me into my first day of school. It would be awkwardly quiet between us with Mum being on edge. Thankfully, school wasn't too far. It was only a twenty-minute drive, although, it seemed unbearably longer given the circumstances.

We reached the school gates, and Mum was happy to have made it here in one piece.

"See, I told you it would be fine."

I think that was her reassuring herself rather than me.

And there it stood, St Bernard's Private School. Its features were enchanting; themed with the French Renaissance era. The main building was riddled with turrets, giving the school the appearance of a mighty chateau.

"Thanks Mum, I'll see you when I finish." I said my goodbyes before slamming the door shut and making my way inside the entrance. As I let down the hood of my jacket, I noticed straight away the long hallway. It looked like a cathedral, there were way too many pillars and the ceiling had inverted, coffered domes. I shook my head in awe and looked for the reception. There behind the desk stood a tall woman.

She met my stare on approaching her and greeted me with a kind smile.

"Hello, are you here to join the first-year induction?"

"Yes, I think so?" I replied, a little confused by her question.

"Well OK, let's see if I can find you," there was an awkward pause, "What's your name, dear?" she prompted.

"Oh sorry, it's Arianna," I replied, feeling

embarrassed to have missed her first cue.

"Arianna, Arianna... Ah yes, here you are. This is your name badge. Please keep it visible; you'll need to join the line ahead and a teacher will be with you soon," she instructed.

"T-thank you," I replied, making sure not to forget my manners.

I joined the back of the line. There were so many students before me; I must have been the last to arrive. Everyone in the line seemed to look as out of place as I felt. It was oddly reassuring. Most had their backs to the wall, and some seemed to have begun already making friends. I saw a few heads peering my way. I guessed that was natural being the newest addition to the queue. It then made sense, the comfort I felt resting my back against the wall, slightly hiding myself behind the bodies in front of me and eradicating any awkward eye contact.

"Hi, Ar-i-anna is it?" The girl in front of me asked, reading my name off my badge.

"Yes, and your name is Ma-la-ya?" I struggled to pronounce it.

"It's actually said as Ma-laya," she corrected.

"Oh, sorry." I blushed.

"It's OK, I get it all the time. I hope the teacher isn't too long now, it's freezing with that big door being open."

"I know, isn't it?" I agreed.

"So, what did you think of the uniform, I mean when you first had to try it on? Isn't it just awful? I mean, who teams up green with purple? These colours aren't great for my undertones, that's for sure." Malaya shared her dislike.

I didn't get what she meant by 'undertones' but I actually like the uniform. It was different. It consisted of:

A dark grey beret hat with a black gloss beak (and purple lining),
A vivid purple and green tie,
A black jumper or cardigan,
A lilac shirt (which is impossible to find anywhere.)
And grey skirt or trousers.

"Hello new day boarders! I hope you're ready for a big day. My name is Mrs Trumpet and I will give you a quick show around before settling you into your house classes."

Mrs Trumpet lead us straight down the hallway and out through the back of the building. The site offered one hundred acres or more according to Mrs Trumpet. It's home to an array of extracurricular activities from clay pigeon shooting, archery, horse riding, cycling, fencing, camping, fishing and jousting to netball, football, basketball, rugby, lacrosse and gymnastics.

Although the list proved to be extensive, I was sold

on signing up for the Girl Guides and Malaya was just as interested. Their base camp wasn't far from the on-sight lake. It looked a little run down, but there was a charming hut attached to the right side of the building. That was where they all hung out after coming back from their adventurous walks within the forest. They'd light up the firepit with the dried-out wood they'd gathered from months before and then cooked up all kinds of food whilst telling scary stories and singing campfire songs. It sounded so amazing. Well, except for the part about having to clean up all the burnt pots and pans afterwards.

Next, Mrs Trumpet led us through the dormitories. This was where all the full boarders stayed. There was a kitchen, a living room with a huge TV, a pool table and shared bedrooms (it must have felt like having sleepovers every night!) Certainly, they offered a comfort away from home. We crossed the bridge which linked the dormitory back to the main building. On either side of the bridge were huge window archways, showing how perfectly the school was perched upon a steep hill, overlooking the nearby town and forest. In my opinion, this was the most beautiful place in the world.

Finally, we reached the end of the show around. Mrs Trumpet began dissecting the year group into their house classes. So far, there were Spartans, Macedonians, Romans and Persians. We seemed to be the last class remaining. I was so relieved to still be alongside Malaya. It would be my kind of luck to make a friend who then ended up not being in any of my classes.

"Right! Here we are. Athenian house. You can all go into the classroom. Mr Judge is waiting for you all."

Mr Judge (I know, right? As if you couldn't have found a more intimidating name). We all made our way into the classroom. It was rather sizable; the décor was panelled from mid-wall to floor in dark-stained mahogany. There was even a risen platform for the teacher to stand on, and that was where Mr Judge stood.

"Welcome Athenians, please come in and take your seats, I'm Mr Judge and I'll be your house teacher."

I have to admit, my first impression of him was as a stern, scary kind of man. He had straight, grey hair that stood on end as though it were fully charged with static. He wore thin, silver-framed glasses that he'd run down his long, crooked nose, revealing the most prolonged, intimidating stare. As the months passed, I noticed this stare would only emerge if he sensed disorder in his class or if you were being difficult. I think this was his tactic to silence the class without having to speak a single word; it had proven to be very effective.

THE STAR SIGNS

Chapter 2

Six months passed, and I'd pleasantly got on well with everyone in Athenian house and in particular the following eleven girls. It's funny to think about it now, but at the time, I didn't have even the tiniest inkling these girls and I would play such a significant role in the near future.

I'll give you a quick introduction.

First there's Malaya. She's a Capricorn, and she always seems to have her nose in a book. Especially if that book is an old history book, reeking of that distinctive 'old book smell.' You could say Malaya was the old soul of the group. You know, the one friend you have who always thinks responsibly. But, on the flip side, she's always the first to explore the fields and climb the tallest things she can find. She's always there to lend a helping hand, and you'd better believe she makes it clear she expects the same in return. She's very fair and level-headed like that.

Chloe is a Gemini. She loves to talk, and she's very popular at school. I believe this is because she's great at mirroring people. It's as though she becomes them. It's remarkable to watch, especially when she's entertaining more than one person at a time. Then you can see how she jumps from one personality to another while remaining true to her own personality, which is witty, fun, and versatile.

Narrisa is a Scorpio, and she joined St Bernard's two months after we did. She's mysterious in her own unique way and has a sarcastic sense of humour. But, then again, she also has a knack for showing her much softer, caring, loving side. Her fashion sense is unorthodox—somewhere between hippie and grunge—and rumour has it, at her old school she once brought in a box of *live* crickets and put them in the school dinners. That's why she moved to St. Bernard's, after being expelled!

Zoe is an Aries and is very honest about her opinion. So much so, she usually says it like it is, which sometimes can come across as a little harsh. I know, though, she doesn't mean it to be the case at all. She's warm-hearted really and wants the best for all her friends. You can count on her to have your back in a sticky situation. She's a loyal friend like that.

Sophia is a Libra and makes friends easily. She is calm and objective. She loves to keep the peace, and she is so organised, she always has the next step already planned out in everything she does. On the other hand, she loves to stir a reaction in the most charming, teasing way, and because of this, she carries her trickery with her wherever she goes.

Charlotte is a Pisces and is always away with the fairies. Well, that's what the teachers tell her, anyway. She loves to create art and she can't help but doodle in class on whatever she has available: scrap pieces of paper, textbooks, desks... even her arms. She must have gotten into trouble over this at least a hundred times within the first months of school. Charlotte never intends to get into trouble; doodling is her way of feeling out all her deepest thoughts.

Ava is a Leo and is passionate when she talks about her interests. She has a warm personality; she likes to clown around, and she's also well spoken. I always refine my speech every time we converse. Ava loves it when the teachers give out presentation homework. She's one of those annoyingly perfect people, who effortlessly gives outstanding presentations every time and without showing any sign of nerves whatsoever.

Amelia is an Aquarius and has a relaxing demeanour, which some people often mistake for a lazy manner. Being so relaxed, she often comes across as not caring about... well, anything, really. However, if you knew her well enough, you'd see she is unapologetically quirky, friendly, and eccentric, with a slightly wicked sense of humour.

Elle is a Virgo and has severely bad OCD; she's forever carrying around disinfectant wipes, cleaning everything she's about to touch. I honestly believe if they allowed her to come into school wearing a complete overall, she would. She's happiest when she can remain in her bubble-like conservativeness. Other than remaining germ free, Elle also likes to keep physically fit and practises healthy eating.

Alicia is a Sagittarius. She is optimistic and has a real knack for electronics. She's always the first one in school to have the latest *thing* going, whether it be the latest phone or the latest pair of socks. Alicia loves to research and analyse and has even dabbled in computer coding (very complicated stuff). Her latest project is blogging. This is where she discusses all her tech jargon and uploads tutorials to help others. She's quite the buff!

Jasmine is a Cancer, and although she can come across as being cold when you first meet her, once she knows she can trust you, she's warm-hearted and protective. She's a lover of poetry and a huge believer in world peace. She's sensitive to her emotions, and the emotions of everyone else. In fact, it's one of the most delightful traits she holds, the ability to place herself in our shoes. Because she's this way inclined, she has a very forgiving, almost motherly, warmth to her.

We were all half-boarders and were all a part of the school Girl Guides.

In the beginning, we acted so differently towards each other. I guess a lot of that was to do with not knowing each other, and our self-conscious feelings about how we'd come across. Not to mention all those nightmarish thoughts of ending up at the bottom of the school food chain, labelled as targets to be picked on throughout the remainder of our school years.

Oh wait! I forgot to tell you about me!

The words 'gentle' and 'friendly' come to mind, being a Taurus. We always have an eccentric chattiness to us. Overall, we are kind, loving people who wear our hearts on our sleeves and are always on a mission for acceptance. On the other hand, we can be extremely stubborn.

Now hold on tight, as this is where things pick up. In fact, make sure you're comfortable because if you're anything like me, you'll find it hard to put this book down.

* * *

DIIIINNGGG!!!!!

I was so happy to hear the home-time bell. I wanted to rush back and tell Mum and Brad all about my day. Even after six months, this was still my daily routine. But as I left the school entrance, I noticed a commotion amongst the other parents. They were rushing around and grabbing their children as they came out of school.

I panicked, even though there was no clear reason. I mean, everyone was panicking, so it seemed like the right thing to do. Suddenly, siren noises were playing across every smartphone in the vicinity at the same time. They were all in sync, as if they were somehow joining to mimic one huge siren. These sirens echoed in my ears as I watched the scene unfold before me.

I then noticed even the full boarders' parents were at the school, demanding to have their children.

Random, scary thoughts filled my mind. Was the world ending? Had aliens landed? What on earth was going on?

Before I knew it, the school entrance became a stampede of frantic parents, searching for and snatching their children away as though their lives depended on it.

I was snatched too.

"Mum!" I yelled. "What's happening?"

"Let's just concentrate on getting home safely, Arianna," Mum replied, her voice shaking a little.

I hurried along with her, unsure of what else to say.

During the car journey home, Mum seemed tense and quiet, and weirdly, she never once asked how my day was, even with all the surrounding commotion. I still couldn't help but feel resentful about that. So, I turned myself towards the window in the hope Mum couldn't read my face (something she's frighteningly good at).

Strangely, the roads seemed a lot calmer than I'd imagined they'd be, at least compared to the chaos of the school rampage. They were a lot quieter than usual for the school rush hour too.

When we arrived home, Mum was in such a rush to stop the car we jolted forwards, parking the car in a highly distressed fashion. Once we were stationary, Mum raced to unclip her seatbelt, trapping one of her most treasured chrome-style false nails between the red release button and the buckle casing as she did so. To my surprise, she didn't seem to care at all. She just ripped her nail out, though still keeping it perfectly intact, without a scratch on it.

When we'd rushed inside, I saw Mum had left the TV on.

Breaking news was appearing on the screen, informing us there was an asteroid within our orbit. The main reason for the commotion was the fact this asteroid was 'like no other we'd ever seen before'. Its estimated size was two hundred feet long. 'Big enough', according to the local news reporter, 'to wipe out the whole of Surrey county'.

As we watched, horrified, the government spoke about several courses of action. They stressed that with the short timescale, it was now too late to respond and that, terrifyingly, the likelihood of impact was inevitable.

I sat down on the sofa, staring at the screen, feeling incredibly numb. The words were going in, but my brain was refusing to believe them. This was too much.

The perfect course of action would have been to launch a nuclear missile to shift its trajectory, which would result in it missing Earth altogether. But the asteroid was now too close to Earth to do anything about it.

Which begged the question: why hadn't this been seen until now? I mean, didn't we have the intelligence and equipment to see these things coming?

Anyway, there was nothing we could do but brace ourselves for impact.

I looked over at Mum, who was staring at me with horror in her eyes. I glanced away quickly, turning my attention back to the screen.

This couldn't be real, could it?

IMPACT

Chapter 3

Mum was cooking my favourite, 'toad in the hole'.

As the smell of oven-cooked sausages and crispy Yorkshire puddings filled the entire house, for a split second I forgot all about the asteroid. We sat down for dinner, and the dining room went quiet as we pushed the food around our plates. That was, except for my brother, Lycan. He was stuffing his little round face as if he hadn't eaten for a decade. It would seem he loved toad in the hole more than I did.

It was now five o'clock in the evening and as pitch-black outside as if it was midnight; the skies were covered in the lowest, thickest clouds I'd ever seen, tainted in an ominous orange glow.

There was a still, eerie feeling in the atmosphere, and I couldn't work out if it was reality or my mind playing tricks on me.

We couldn't help but be on edge.

Wanting to break the silence, Mum switched on the TV again, seeing if there were any further updates. The news anchor told us everything about the asteroid was 'unpredictable', from 'its activity to its probable size'. He was interviewing an asteroid expert, Drayson Black, who was the senior chief scientist for the UK Space Agency. According to his studies, the asteroid was 'already vaporising' and was 'currently stationary'. He expressed there wasn't 'a logical reason this should happen as this behaviour wasn't normal for an asteroid'. Asteroids usually vaporised once they'd entered a planet's atmosphere.

The news of Drayson Black's findings felt like a slight relief, knowing the asteroid was already stopped in its tracks and falling apart, but one thing was certain. This asteroid was 'an unpredictable threat'.

An additional baffling thought was this asteroid wasn't your usual charcoal grey colour. Why did that matter? Well, as Drayson Black explained, their colour was usually the reason it was so hard to detect asteroids further afield. Because of their camouflaged behaviour, it was like finding a 'needle in a haystack'.

This explanation would have made perfect sense why we'd overlooked this asteroid, although it was still unlikely because of its sheer size and not forgetting its vivid colouring.

The press pictures released by the UK Space Agency showed the asteroid's marvellous burnt orange colour, which made it luminous within the galactic darkness. It was beautiful and striking in its appearance. Its shape was uniquely formed with rough, irregular surfaces housing dense, razor-like stacks, which made up half the asteroid's overall size. I imagined the terrain of Mars to look similar.

Drayson Black mentioned the asteroid was likely to comprise of mostly minerals including iron, copper, platinum, and gold, and less valuable properties such as clay and space dust. They called this asteroid 'metallic' because of its higher than usual volume of precious metals. This would explain its reflective surface, though it instilled further fear. It would also make the asteroid a lot heavier and harder to break up on its way down. The density and angle of the asteroid were the worst combination you could ask for. Things were looking bad at this point.

They even predicted it would hit somewhere around Europe, going from Iceland all the way over to Russia. The news then showed a map of the world, marking the area with a red circle.

Wait a minute! Now, I was no Einstein when it comes to geography, but even I knew England was within this circle—the harsh, thick red line was telling us we'd get hit with the full impact. Even if it hit the furthest point away from us within that scary red circle, we would still experience the fatal aftermath of airbursts, earthquakes, ash clouds, fires, and tsunamis.

At this realisation, I burst into uncontrollable tears, causing Mum to leap forward and bring me in for a cuddle. I was so overwhelmed with all the dramatic changes and the potential mass devastation, which, in case I needed to remind you, would happen within less than twenty-four-hours. I could no longer cope with all the floods of horrifying information.

As seven o'clock approached, there was a change in the atmosphere. Suddenly, it started pouring down with what sounded like a continuous bucketful of water emptying upon the house, as though the rain was entertaining a furious thunderstorm.

Once Mum made her way downstairs after putting Lycan to bed, she and Brad started making phone calls. I could see Brad's face laced with eagerness to hear a voice pick up on the other end of the line. However, his enthusiasm was untimely, as Mum got through first.

"I need to book your next available flight for two adults and two children, anywhere outside of Europe," she gasped.

"I'm sorry, Ma'am," the airline operator replied over the speakerphone, "but due to the adverse weather conditions all flights have been cancelled until further notice."

Mum swiftly hung up and tried another, the two of them continuing this for a good hour or so with every airport and airline they could think of. Out of desperation, they even tried contacting a private helicopter, which would have cost them thousands, but still no luck. It seemed this weather had trapped us all, sealing our fate.

After hanging up the phone on her final attempt, Mum collapsed on the edge of our pewter-coloured, crushed velvet sofa, holding her head in her hands.

"It's just hopeless!" she cried.

Placing a reassuring hand on her arm, Brad suggested we all watch a movie to take our minds off the disaster. After all, there *was* a chance we'd all be ok. I mean, they could have had the asteroid's trajectory all wrong. Perhaps it wouldn't even hit Earth and would instead vaporise before it could hit the ground.

I guess when all else fails, all we have to hold on to is hope.

So, we sat down and watched the movie premiere of the famous musical, *The Rose of Hope*. We'd been meaning to watch this for ages, so it was a delight to see it airing on TV. I hoped it would be the kind of movie we needed to pick us up. I noticed, however,

Brad was making out he wanted to watch it so we wouldn't be trying to pick a movie forever, (which was what usually happened). He's great like that.

Before the film started, I went to the kitchen to see what goodies we had in the snack cupboard. Mum allocated this tiny cupboard solely for heavenly junk food, so she wouldn't be easily tempted to snack on it all the time. I mean, it's a great idea, just not so great when I have to climb on the countertop to reach it.

After deciding between the space dippers, croc 'o' jacks, Carlisle's soured drops and penny gels; I grabbed the popcorn. I hopped back down and peered through the condensation resting on the kitchen window.

Outside in the garden, I thought I saw an egg-shaped boulder smouldering on the lawn in front of our Buxus sempervirens shrubs at the end of the garden. Deep orange lava-like veins seemed to run down the object, whatever it was.

Blinking hard, I wiped the condensation from the window only to reveal there was nothing there.

"But it looked completely real!" I stated to myself, bewildered, before adding, "Oh great, now I'm hallucinating!" I shook my head, sighing. I needed to relax.

I made my way back to the living room in time for the start of the movie, then I made myself all snug with my fluffy rainbow blanket before tucking into my sweet and salty popcorn.

BUZZZZZ!

My phone went off, immediately waking me up. I must have fallen asleep.

I glanced over at Mum and Brad to see they'd also fallen fast asleep, then I looked at the TV. The movie had finished. I didn't even remember watching most of it.

I grabbed my phone to see why it was vibrating and found it nestled under a mound of wasted popcorn, which I must have spilt whilst tossing in my sleep.

It was the 'Girl Guides' group chat, which consisted of all twelve of us girls. Opening the chat to see I'd missed the start of the conversation, I scrolled up to read what was going on.

Girl Guides Chat
Friday

Jasmine
At 01:25am: "Girls, are you all OK?"

Charlotte
At 01:32am: "OMG, what happened??"

Jasmine
At 01:34am: "I think it just disappeared!"

Charlotte

At 01:35am: "How is that possible?"

Elle

At 01:36am: "Hey guys, I felt something... my bedroom was shaking."

Narrisa

At 01:38am: "Mine too! And I saw something bright pass my window... I think something landed there in the field."

Narrisa

At 01:40am: "Let's go and check it out!"

Malaya

At 01:44am: "Narrisa, I don't think that's a good idea. We don't even know what it is... Something doesn't feel right."

Elle

At 01:50am: "Malaya's right, for all we know it could be dangerous and we could be exposed to loads of harmful stuff... like space disease!"

Narrisa

At 01.51am: "Space disease? Is that even a thing?"

Elle

At 01:55am: "*Rolling eyes*"

Alicia

At 02:00am: "Hey guys, I'm OK. Where are all the other girlies?... Girls, tell us you're all OK!"

Chloe

At 02:01am: "I'm OK."

Sophia

At 02:01am: "Me too."

Ava

At 02:02am: "And me."

Zoe

At 02:04am: "I'm good."

Arianna

At 02:05am: "I'm here."

Amelia

At 02:05am: "I'm OK too, so what are we doing?"

Narrisa

At 02:08am: "Something landed in the fields behind my house. I think it's to do with the asteroid. I'm going to go and have a look. Whoever wants to come with me, be at mine in 30 mins."

I sat back in my seat to process what I should do, but to be honest, I'd *no idea* what to do.

If I didn't go and all the other girls did, I would miss out on something awesome! And I didn't want to be the only one who didn't show up. I mean, I didn't think I'd look like such a great friend if I didn't go. Besides, Narrisa's house was only a ten-minute walk from my house. None of my family would even know I was gone.

I turned over the channel on the TV to see if the news had any updates, but nothing was airing; it was just static on every channel. *Strange!*

Next I went on the internet on my phone and searched for asteroid updates, but they'd mentioned nothing new for a while.

Forget this, I thought, *I'm going*. It wasn't like I'd be able to get back to sleep with all this going on anyway.

Carefully, I eased myself off the sofa, trying to be quiet so I wouldn't wake up Mum and Brad. I crept out of the living room and rushed upstairs, quickly checking on Lycan to see if he was still fast asleep. He was. After entering my pastel purple-themed bedroom,

I picked up my grey faded hoodie and my Converse shoes and threw them on.

Sneaking back downstairs, I peered from the hallway into the living room to check the coast was clear, then I made my way to the front door, letting myself out.

THE MEETUP

Chapter 4

The streetlights were out, and in the darkness, I couldn't even see my hand in front of my face. I patted down my pockets to fetch my phone and switched on the torchlight.

I hate the dark. My mind always plays tricks on me. I make out strange, almost demonic-looking faces in nearby objects. And I don't know if it's just me, but whenever I'm alone in the dark, I always feel like there's someone behind me. It's so creepy!

What makes it worse is the fact I live in a wooded

commuter town in northern Surrey, where wildlife is in abundance. This means I could unknowingly walk up to a deer, a fox, a huge badger, or a hedgehog. Well, I wouldn't mind the hedgehogs; they aren't so bad.

The nearby owl I could hear wit-wooing wasn't helping to set a less creepy mood either.

Scattered puddles filled the pavements and, because the lighting was so bad, I would try to miss one only to end up clumsily jumping in another. To top it all off, I was wearing the most inappropriate shoes. "I should have put on my boots and not these Chucks!" I muttered to myself. My socks were already soaked, and I was only a few metres down the street.

What's that? I thought, having heard some rustling sounds and what seemed to be footsteps somewhere in front of me. *I wish these phone lights were more powerful!* I couldn't see that far ahead. All I could make out was there was someone walking, so I immediately slowed down.

This, however, was in vain, as the person still turned around, shining their phone light back at me.

"Err... he-hello?" I asked nervously, awaiting a reply.

"Arianna, is that you?" came a voice from behind the light.

"Yes... Sophia, is that you?" I replied, puzzled.

Slowly, we edged towards one another.

"OMG, you scared the life out of me, creeping up

on me like that!" Sophia gasped, slightly breathless as she held her hand over her chest.

"I could say the same thing!" I replied, relieved.

We continued our journey to Narrisa's house together, and I felt more confident now I wasn't travelling alone in the darkness.

"So, is this asteroid not up there anymore or what?" questioned Sophia.

"I have no clue!" I replied, shrugging. "None of the TV channels are working anymore, and when I searched the internet, there was nothing new mentioned."

"It's so strange. I'm curious to see if there *is* anything behind Narrisa's house. Do you think she might be making it up?" Sophia asked me quietly.

"I did think that… but then Elle said it first, about her room shaking…" I reminded her.

"That's true," Sophia agreed. "Come on, let's hurry up and find out."

When we got to Narrisa's house, there wasn't any time to waste. The other girls were already standing there with their phone torches on, ready to explore the site where this unknown object had possibly crash-landed.

Together, we made our way over there.

The fields behind Narrisa's house were the beginning line of the forest that backed onto the acres of land belonging to the school we all attended.

"I wonder what it is," whispered Ava excitedly.

"It could be nothing," Malaya pointed out.

"I just hope we don't come to regret this..." said Elle, before placing her mouth mask on.

"What's that?" asked Narrisa, intrigued.

"It's a respirator to protect me from airborne viruses and diseases," said Elle proudly, though there was a slight defensive tone to her voice.

"OK..." replied Narrisa slowly, puzzled.

We were now entering the field. The pasture was the size of a football pitch, and it was drenched in water that accumulated from the rainfall earlier.

As we were slushing along towards the tree border, all I could think of was the alibi I'd have to come up with for this. I'd have to explain to my parents where my new shoes had disappeared to; there was no chance I would turn up at home with these filthy Chucks.

We'd now entered the woodland area, which was usually teeming with life. On this occasion it was still and silent... almost as if we were in a foreign place, somewhere unfamiliar to us. The only noises we could hear were the squelching sounds coming from our shoes and the overemphasised breathing coming from Elle's respirator.

The ground here was a lot drier than the field, the trees placed spaciously apart, with ivy climbing upward from their bases and encasing their elongated branches.

There was still a slight tinge of orange light in the air, which grew brighter as we edged nearer to the sighting. Even the pleasant smell of wet earth was now morphing into the most putrid stench of rotten eggs.

"Ew, can anyone else smell that?" Jasmine asked, pinching her nose closed.

"Yes, it smells like a fart!" giggled Charlotte.

"I'd have that looked at, if your farts smell that bad." Amelia laughed.

"I was obviously joking," said Charlotte, a little defensively.

As the trees thinned out, the amber light burned ever so brightly, calmly and consecutively pulsating from a weaker current to a stronger one.

We were now entering the clearing. The grass was much longer here, and as it couldn't support its own length, it buckled upon itself, creating bumpy mounds—a huge difference to the perfectly formed field we'd started in. It was still pitch-black, which was normal for three o'clock in the morning, yet somehow it felt even darker than usual.

You could feel the nervousness surrounding our group, no one having spoken for the past five-minutes. We'd even changed from walking in a loose group to moving in a tight one, practically shoulder to shoulder, as though we were all having to squeeze through the tiniest gap at once.

We continued to venture from the breaking of the

trees towards the middle of the clearing, peering into the gloom.

Out there, vaguely, in the distance, was the reason for that pulsating, amber light.

THE ORB

Chapter 5

As we were standing in the clearing, dark clouds started swirling above us. They were low, touching the treetops bordering the clearing, and they were all moving in formation as though they were attempting to produce a tornado. A slight tail formed above the amber beacon.

Oddly, the wind around us was swirling in the opposite direction to the corresponding scenery above us. The force was strong enough to flatten the leaves against the bark of the trees.

It now contained us in some kind of turbulent, makeshift room, and it felt like we were dreaming; the events unfolding before us were not of this world.

"We really shouldn't be here," stated Malaya.

"Let's turn back. We've seen enough!" agreed Chloe, stopping in her tracks.

"For Pete's sake!" cried Narrisa. "We can't turn back now; we're nearly there. Don't you want to see what it is?"

"Let's just get close enough to see a little clearer… then we can leave," Sophia suggested.

We edged cautiously closer until we were about two hundred metres in front of the amber light. It was then an image appeared behind the hue. It was an egg-shaped object that hovered up and down as if to show us our Earth's gravity didn't affect it. The surface appeared flawlessly smooth and raging hot, the dispersing heat was so intense it distorted the image of the egg-shaped boulder. We could feel the heat warming the front of our bodies, whilst behind us it was much cooler and windier. It was hard to determine the size of the boulder as it was hovering, but I'd gauge it was slightly smaller than me—about five foot.

"Wow, I don't think this is an asteroid *at all!*" stated Alicia.

Zoe was staring at it in awe. "What else could it be?"

"This is so amazing!" exclaimed Sophia.

"I've seen this before..." I blurted, thinking back to earlier.

"Really, Arianna? Where?" asked Ava, intrigued.

"Earlier on, when I was at home..." I replied, butterflies appearing in my tummy as I cast my mind back. Why had I seen this exact boulder in my garden earlier? Was it a premonition? Had someone—or something—been trying to warn me? What if it was trying to tell me something important, and I just didn't understand what it was?

"*No, Narrisa, stop!*" shouted Elle suddenly.

We all gasped as Narrisa confidently grabbed a nearby rock, which was slightly larger than her fist, and threw it with all her strength towards the floating, egg-shaped boulder. Her aim was so accurate, it hit the object right in the middle.

For a split second, it seemed to have had no impact; the rock bounced back off and landed on the nearby grass, smouldering away and further confirming the intense heat the boulder was emitting.

"Narrisa, why would you endanger us all like that?" Malaya demanded.

"You're so lucky nothing happened!" I added.

"Oh, cool down, I knew nothing would happen!" Narrisa shot back defensively.

Suddenly, the nature of the boulder changed. We could see it was now reacting to the disturbance Narrisa caused. Immediately, the boulder stopped hovering in mid-air and started shuddering as the smooth surface cracked open like an egg hatching, the cracking sounds hugely amplified. Then, as we watched in shock, lava-like veins flowed in place of the cracks. Just like the hallucination I saw earlier; now it was clear that it was a warning.

Our collective instinct was to run away before things got really bad, but we couldn't move. It was as though a great force of gravity turned the weight of our bodies into solid lead. We were being prevented from escaping and all we could do was helplessly wait, petrified for what was to come.

The shudders became more turbulent as the object started shaking from side to side.

At this point I was certain it would explode, but it stopped and projected a blinding spectrum of light. It beamed towards us in twelve individual rays, gently penetrating our chests. In the next moment gravity left our bodies as we elevated effortlessly off the ground in a similar motion to the egg-shaped boulder.

The sensation was magical. I felt an immediate rush of happiness and an immense, powerful energy flowing through my body. I looked over to my left to see Amelia staring at me, smiling as we were lifted upwards. She was trying to speak to me, but I couldn't hear anything. I could tell from the look on her face she felt the same as I did.

This tranquil experience, however, was about to

end.

First our hearing returned, and then…

VOOM!

A deafening sound pierced our eardrums as the egg-shaped boulder burst open, propelling razor-sharp fragments toward us. Once they entered the stream of light created by the rays, the fragments gathered enormous speed. They resembled oversized rocky splinters, and they were now darting straight towards our chests.

A sharp, burning sensation overwhelmed our torsos, and we reacted in the only way we could— by wailing in extreme pain as the fragments impaled our chests. This traumatic experience ended with the production of several blazing shockwaves, sending us hurtling backwards.

Gravity returned to our bodies then, resulting in us crashing into the ground with brutal force.

We lay there unconscious for a moment, and just like that, the once highly turbulent clearing was now still and lifeless.

AFTERMATH

Chapter 6

I finally awoke after what must have been hours, my back stiff and my head pounding. I tried to rub the soreness out of my eyes in the hope it would help ease them open. When they did my eyesight was so blurry, I tried to regain my vision by focusing on the night sky. When the view finally came into focus, I could see the stars prominently dotted around like little specks of silvery glitter. It was as though someone had taken the time to individually separate them and intricately place them against the emptiness of the black night sky.

Relaxing, I took a moment to view them. I was certain I could see pictures forming. Could they be related to the constellations? I only questioned myself because I remember Mum once showing me Orion's Belt one evening, but this time it was different. It looked so clear I could see faint lines running between the stars, mapping out the images and instantly reminding me of a dot-to-dot picture.

I could now sense dawn approaching. It was as though there was an internal alarm notifying me, so I went to grab my phone from my jacket pocket to see how late it was. The screen, however, was in bits. In fact, it was completely obliterated!

It dawned on me then how powerful the impact had been (from which we'd somehow survived). But honestly, how *had* we survived? Surely an impact of that magnitude should have gravely injured us, or worse... killed us.

Intense flashbacks flooded my mind, filled with all the pain and screaming we'd endured. It made me shudder.

As I gently rubbed my chest to reassure myself, I stumbled across a scabby oval bump, placed right in the centre of my chest. My heart raced as I traced its shape. It rose in the centre before levelling back out at the edges, merging with my body as though they were one. Looking down, it horrified me to see one fragment from earlier, which I now recall darting towards us, was embedded into my chest.

I tried to pick it off, but the scab remained stubbornly in place.

Screaming aloud in fear, I jumped to my feet with one last desperate attempt to brush it off me. There was no pain in my chest, nothing compared to the excruciating pain I'd felt earlier.

I glanced around me to see where the other girls were.

They'd all awoken too, and judging from the head holding and back stretching, we were all feeling the same strange soreness.

We'd all fallen uniformly around the remains of the boulder, of which only the bottom half survived. There was an enormous burnt ring on the ground around us where the overgrown grass had once been. The luscious green surroundings were now caked in thick black soot and the last of the burning embers.

"Ouch, I can't move my arm!" cried Amelia. She was bent over in agony, holding her left arm against her torso with her right.

The rest of us were now up on our feet, rushing over to see what was wrong, and once we were by her side, we could examine her state of wellbeing. The left arm of her tracksuit was burnt and torn up to the shoulder, perfectly exposing her injury. There were no visible burns, just black smudges from the charred sleeve.

"Oh, that looks painful, Amelia," I said, confirming the damage.

Her forearm, bruised purple and disfigured by the swelling, indicated a likely fracture.

"What should we do?" Chloe asked in a panic.

"Alicia, you're the Girl Guides' first aider. What do we do?" asked Zoe.

"Well, it definitely looks bad. Maybe we should get help," Alicia suggested. "Amelia, can you move your arm at all?"

"No!" sobbed Amelia.

"OK, stay still. Me and Narrisa will go get help," Alicia reassured her. "You guys, stay here."

"But who will you get? We're gonna be in so much trouble!" exclaimed Chloe.

"That's true," Alicia agreed, sighing. "Well, does anyone else have a solution?"

We spent a moment throwing around ideas on the best course of action. Meanwhile, to help ease her shaking, Charlotte and Jasmine gathered some cindered wood to start a miniature fire on the burnt soil near Amelia.

Narrisa placed her thick woolly cardigan (which she'd been wearing under her duffle jacket) over Amelia. As her hand touched Amelia's arm, a gentle golden light beamed out from the palm of Narrisa's hand, causing her to jump back in shock.

"What the heck was that?" shouted Narrisa.

"What happened?" I questioned.

"A golden light just came out of my hand!" explained Narrisa, sounding slightly hysterical. "Look, I'll try and do it again!"

As we all gathered around to watch, Narrisa placed her hand gently in the same position as before, hovering over Amelia's damaged arm. Once again, a brilliant golden beam expelled out from her palm. The beam then expanded, wrapping itself around Amelia's arm and pulsated. Within seconds her arm seemed to improve, the ordinary colour returned, and the swelling vanished.

"This is so cool! It's healing my arm," Amelia shouted in excitement.

"What? How?" Sophia replied, baffled.

A moment later Narrisa's hand stopped emitting the golden beam and Alicia could move her arm freely once again.

"Oh, Narrisa, thank you!" Amelia said gratefully.

"OK, I'm officially freaking out!" shouted Sophia. "What is this? What's happened to us?"

"It must have something to do with these scabs. You guys all have this as well, right?" I asked, intrigued, as I revealed the oval scab attached to my sternum. Judging from the mortified looks on the girls' faces, they'd only just realised the same oval scabby fragment was embedded in their chests too.

Screaming was also their reaction.

"Why won't it come off? Surely it has to come off?" Ava cried frustratingly.

"It won't, I've tried already," I stated, trying to remain calm.

"How bizarre is it that we all have the same identical scab in the exact same place?" asked Chloe.

"I was just thinking the same thing!" agreed Zoe.

"Guys, we better get back home before our parents wake up," Chloe forewarned.

"Agreed! And we probably shouldn't mention any of this to *anyone!*" added Elle. "At least not until we know more."

We all agreed with Elle. I mean, we would be in so much trouble, and we'd definitely be grounded if our parents found out where we'd been. Plus, I honestly didn't want to ruin my chances of going on the upcoming school trip. We were going to the National Space Centre next week. I've been excited about it for a whole month.

And so, we all rushed out of the clearing, headed through the woods, and made our way back home.

As I entered the front door of my house, Mum and Brad were still both 'out like a light' on the sofa. What a relief!

After gently closing the door, I made my way up the stairs. It helped that by now I'd figured out the precise pressure and position with which to place my feet on each step to avoid making any sound. In fact, I always felt a sense of pride by the time I reached the final step without being heard.

Rushing to my bedroom, I got changed into my pyjamas and then hid my filthy, tattered clothes by wedging them between the wall and my bed.

When I looked at my alarm clock, I couldn't believe it was now six in the morning. Where had the last hour gone? I had to work fast.

I rushed to the bathroom and grabbed my facecloth. You should have seen the state of me! I looked like I'd fallen down a chimney! But it was way too early to be having a shower, and it would raise suspicion if my parents noticed. Instead, I began frantically scrubbing at my skin with the damp cloth, unable to understand how there weren't any grazes or bloodstains, especially around the scab on my chest. I focused, peering closer into the mirror; I noticed a break in the centre of the scab, but I didn't want to force it open. I wasn't ready to see what was hiding underneath.

I could hear the house beginning to wake up, so I crept back out and finally jumped into my warm, welcoming bed.

As soon as my head landed on the plush, overfilled pillow, I was 'out for the count'.

OATH

Chapter 7

"Why am I in the clearing again?" I announced, puzzled.

I'd found myself right back inside the burnt circle, alongside the remains of the boulder, exactly as we'd left it.

I looked around and realised it was just me here. With a sinking feeling in my gut, I panicked and ran out of the clearing. I entered the forest and started zipping through the trees, only to end up right back where I'd started.

"What's going on? I must be dreaming," I said to myself.

"Yes, you are dreaming," a gentle, female, stellar kind of voice confirmed.

I jumped and frantically looking around to see who it was, but yet again, there was no one in sight. Who did the voice belong to? It was so unfamiliar.

"Who... who are you?" I asked.

"My name is Ethereal, and I am your celestial guardian," announced the unknown voice.

"Celestial guardian?" I repeated, puzzled.

"I'm sure you're confused with everything that's occurred over the last twenty-four hours, Arianna, but I am here now to explain exactly what happened."

"OK," I replied. I think I was in shock, but I wanted to know what was going on.

"However, before I explain, I need you to peer over the remains of the boulder," instructed Ethereal.

I felt equal amounts of hesitation and eagerness, which made my body move in several directions. I was in a complete muddle.

Eventually I kneeled down before the boulder, hesitantly placing both my hands either side of its exposed edges before leaning forward.

As I did so, a familiar spectrum of light shone up towards me, making me gasp. The beauty within this boulder was immense. The entire inside was covered in sparkling crystals, packed tightly together, with each crystal containing its own hue of the rainbow.

"Oh, wow, this is so beautiful!" I said in awe.

"Now, don't be alarmed by what happens next," warned Ethereal.

"Huh?" I responded.

Just then, colourful water began filling the boulder, submerging the crystals and immediately making the boulder look far larger than before.

"Is it getting bigger?" I asked. "Or am I tilting closer?"

The next thing I knew, I was falling in, spiralling amongst the blur as the echoes of my screams chased behind me.

Suddenly, I appeared in unfamiliar territory. It seemed I'd been teleported to another, unearthly place. I stood there feeling exposed.

"Arianna, I am now going to show you what this boulder means," continued Ethereal. "Its origin is a planet called Zodiac."

I scanned around me, as she spoke; looking for some kind of clarification on who or what she was. But the only thing to appear was a veil, it seemed to be showing me a planet I've never seen before.

"Zodiac is like Earth—it is, in fact, Earth's parallel—sharing the same map of constellations. But extraordinarily, these two planets are placed billions of light years apart, Zodiac with its own astronomical climate that harbours its own unique life source.

Although there are many similarities between Earth and Zodiac, they also have many differences," she carried on. "Zodiac is ruled equally by two very different beings. They are called Empearions and Argonauts, these beings are continuously plagued by the feuds of their venomous pasts."

Venomous pasts? What was going on here?

"Over the centuries, they remained unable to form any treaty between them, and as a result; the great battle took place, ruining the lands of Argon."

Ethereal's voice began to echo-out. I shut my eyes, cupping my hands either side of my head; in an effort to re-focus on her voice. It seemed to be working.

"After the great battle. Argon was changed forever. What remains now are dark burnt soils, laced in death, placed below murky green skies. The Argonauts had no choice but to venture deeper within Zodiac and today, Argon is made up of underground surface layers, ruled by the Argonauts. The Empearions inhabit the other half of Zodiac. Their lands having remained untouched are now flourishing with white marble buildings surrounded by luscious nature."

I frowned, uncertain what it meant.

"The boulder you have come to know is from Zodiac. It is not an asteroid but only a vessel for twelve powerfully charged Birthstones; each one carries its own gifts. These Birthstones are untainted from the vicious environment they once called home. None of this was by chance, Arianna. All twelve of you have been chosen; Earth was chosen."

My mouth dropped open. *Chosen for what?*

"But heed this: 'Remember to be kind, to empower, and most of all to always be the source of light in which shadows fall behind.' Do you take this oath, Arianna?"

"I promise," I replied, not able to place exactly what I was promising and still feeling completely bewildered but knowing, somehow, I must trust Ethereal. What else was I meant to do?

"Perfect! Now, about the scab on your chest. It will start to heal and as it does, you will become regenerative. But it probably won't heal as you'd hope," Ethereal explained. "What I mean to say is, it will leave behind a special mark—your chosen Birthstone. Yes, that's right, Arianna, the Birthstone will remain within your body."

Perhaps she could tell from my expression how confused, not to mention frightened, I was.

"You see, these precious Birthstones always need to be carried in some kind of vessel. If they were to somehow become host-less… well, that would be a whole other conundrum. So, remember to always look after them. The Birthstones are meant to be used for justice, but in the wrong soul, they would cause great peril. Now, we've run out of time. You will hear from me again, but only when you truly need my assistance," ended Ethereal, smiling. "Goodbye, Arianna."

THE DAY THAT FOLLOWED

Chapter 8

I was puzzled. Utterly puzzled! That's the only way I could describe the past day's events as they played over and over again in my mind.

I tucked into my strawberry jam toast, which has been a long-time breakfast favourite of mine, and as I chewed, I pondered a little more.

"Had a rough night's sleep?" asked Brad.

"You could say that," I replied.

"Is it because of your chest?" he then questioned.

"Uh, what?" I jumped out from my deep thoughts.

"Wow, calm down. I was only asking because you've been rubbing your chest ever since you've sat down for breakfast," he explained.

"Oh yeah, I have a little heartburn." Relieved, I immediately stopped rubbing my chest.

The sound from the TV increased as Mum turned up the volume.

"No one seems to know what happened to the mysterious 'object' that wreaked havoc yesterday," the TV news presenter was saying. "Was it, in fact, an asteroid? Or was it some kind of hoax? Well, Drayson Black is here to shed some light on the matter."

I focused on the screen.

"Mr Black, thank you for agreeing to come on air once again," the news presenter continued. "Could you please explain exactly what happened to this 'asteroid'?"

"Good morning. Y-yes, of course," Drayson Black replied. "Well, I've been up all night re-analysing my findings, and it seems that… well, hidden behind the asteroid was a black hole which must have swallowed up the asteroid and then itself."

The news presenter's jaw dropped open in disbelief. "Ahem," she mumbled, shaking herself back into focus. "Do you have any visual evidence of this you can show us now?"

"N-no," stuttered Drayson Black. "I wasn't informed I'd have to provide any of my research. To be honest, I'm just as baffled as everyone else." He laughed a little, shaking his head. "I'm afraid I need more time to analyse all the evidence I've gathered."

"The viewers need to know more than that, Mr Black," persisted the presenter. "Can you elaborate any further?"

"At this moment in time, I can't say any more than what I've already told you," reaffirmed Drayson Black, who by now was looking mildly uncomfortable.

"Was there *really* an asteroid?" the news presenter continued, hurling another question at him.

"Ha... well, there was definitely *something* there, though whether it was an asteroid or something else, I simply don't know yet," Drayson Black responded. He appeared a little insulted.

"Right, that's all we have time for. Thank you, Mr Black," the news presenter concluded, not looking at all thankful for his input. The camera then closed in on her as she said, "Is it possible to be left more confused? Well, thanks to the 'experts', we may never know what happened to the mystery asteroid. If, in fact, that's what it was. For now, I'll have to leave that for you to decide."

I was so relieved there was no mention of the orb. I knew more than everyone else, but I still wished I'd asked Ethereal more questions in my dream, or whatever it was. I mean, what the heck are a bunch of twelve-year-old girls supposed to do with these ultimate power stones? And besides, no one even asked me if I wanted to be a part of this. No one asked any of us.

Luckily, Mum and Brad didn't suspect anything about last night's escapades. If they did, surely, I'd already be grounded, and with a space rock in my chest to boot.

Wondering if any of the other girls experienced a strange dream, I opened the chat and began a conversation.

Girl Guides Chat
Saturday

Arianna
At 10:26am: "Hey girls, shall we meet up?"

Jasmine
At 10:29am: "Hey, at the usual place?"

Arianna
At 10:32am: "Be there for 12?"

We have our own pretty cool secret hangout, a shelter-type place we'd stumbled across during one of our Girl Guides' walks. It was nestled amongst the trees, hidden beneath overgrown weeds and littered with hollow branches. I think it was used for safety centuries ago, like those Stanton shelters built to protect civilians from air raids back in World War Two. They'd concealed the entire shelter underneath with several layers of soil.

The place had a worn-out, bricked, boarded entrance that revealed five generously sized steps leading down into a single empty room. They made the walls with reinforced concrete, reaching up to at least seven feet in height. It was large enough to accommodate all twelve of us at once, with some wiggle room left over. We'd decked it all out in our own style of makeshift furnishings, and we'd even donated some of our old furniture to make it cosy. It got cold in there, as you can probably imagine, so we'd piled a load of blankets in there too.

I arrived at the shelter at exactly twelve o'clock to find everyone else already there. I guessed I wasn't the only one wanting to get something off my chest (figuratively speaking).

"Hey," I said, before launching straight into it. "I had such a strange dream last night…"

"So did I…" the girls replied all at once, confused.

"What? About Zodiac, Ethereal, the Empearions and the Argonauts?" I asked, not even stopping for breath.

Slowly, the girls nodded.

We all looked at each other in utter amazement. Could we all have experienced the same dream? Seriously? And, what did Ethereal mean by we've 'all been chosen'? I mean, how had we been chosen? And why had we been chosen?

"We should compare notes," I said, after a few moments of silence.

We ended up hanging out in our shelter for far longer than we'd intended, going over everything that happened and getting a load off our minds. It was reassuring, and we felt so much closer to one another than we'd ever felt before.

"So, what now?" asked Amelia, when there was a lull in the conversation.

"Don't know. I guess we just wait and see what happens?" replied Charlotte, shrugging.

"No, we can't just wait it out!" Narrisa exclaimed in disagreement. "You heard what Ethereal said. We have to learn to control our powers."

"But how can we do that, when we haven't even seen any evidence of powers yet?" questioned Jasmine. "So far, Narrisa's the only one who's done anything."

"Jasmine has a point," agreed Zoe. "Maybe we should go back to the clearing and see what's happened to the boulder?"

It was a great idea, as the boulder was in the next clearing along from our hideout. I wanted to see if it was still as vividly coloured as I recalled in my dream, and I was also a little curious to see if anything else would happen. Would Ethereal return once more? Somehow, in the back of my mind, I knew this boulder still had a relevant part to play in whatever was going on.

When we entered the clearing, the first thing we noticed was the black soot from the explosion had disappeared, returning the surroundings to their usual luscious green state. Even the burnt ring surrounding the boulder had vanished. It was as though nothing life-changing or turbulent had happened here. The only thing that remained was the broken boulder.

It was mostly as I remembered, but there was something amiss. The marvellous crystals with their sparkly rainbow hues were now dull looking. It almost seemed like the boulder was trying to camouflage itself to protect it from being noticed.

We decided it was best to hide the boulder as its unique formation was still noticeable to the human eye. We gathered everything we could find; dirt, soil, fallen leaves, twigs, and sticks, and arranged them around it, trying to make it look natural.

"That'll do for now," I said, admiring our handiwork.

I hoped that was true.

STRANGE THINGS

Chapter 9

Oh, how I despised food tech class. I couldn't stand these lessons of pointlessly cooking food!

Fortunately, Mrs Battenberg was our food tech teacher, a motherly, caring type of woman full of joy and very bubbly which made food tech lessons bearable, at least.

She favoured long, chequered-styled dresses which always seemed to be two sizes too small for her somewhat curvaceous figure. She always wore her grown-out, rooted with greys, brunette hair loosely plaited and styled in a double Dutch braided bun. I was convinced she started the week with a fresh plait on Monday and left it in all week. You could see it deteriorating as the days rolled by, and once Friday appeared, her hair was in such a frayed state it was unbelievable. Mrs Battenberg also loved to wear the colour red on her thinly stretched lips, and on most of her teeth too.

"Right," announced Mrs Battenberg, "in today's lesson we'll be making apple crumble. Come over and watch, quickly! I'm going to demonstrate, then you'll go off and repeat what I've shown you. Remember, you must take notes; there will be an essay on this."

Out of our Girl Guides group there were six of us in this food tech class: me, Elle, Sophia, Chloe, Jasmine, and Amelia.

She paired me with Sophia, which was mutually agreeable for us both as I hated to cook, but Sophia loved it. Honestly, if I wasn't going to be marked down for not participating in the cooking part, I would happily sit back and let Sophia do the whole thing. I'd be there as the food taster. You know, making sure everything was seasoned well.

It was now our turn to repeat what Mrs Battenberg showed us, so we got going straight away with peeling the apples. Another reason I detest cooking.

Lo-and-behold, I snagged the one peeler that was on the fritz. Just my luck! I think a spoon would have been sharper.

Sophia, on the other hand, was effortlessly and confidently peeling her way through the bunch of apples as though she'd been working in a kitchen for years.

I got so frustrated with my peeler I dug it right into the apple and gave one big tug towards my thumb. "*Ouch!*" I shouted, grabbing my thumb tightly.

"What happened?" Sophia asked with concern.

"Arianna, is everything OK over there?" questioned Mrs Battenberg.

I looked down at my bleeding thumb as it started throbbing, while Mrs Battenberg made her way across the classroom to see if I was OK. I looked up at her, and when I noticed the pain disappear suddenly, I glanced back down at my thumb. There was still a significant amount of blood, but now there was no more pain and no cut. Quickly, I washed the blood from my hands, so the teacher wouldn't be startled. I suspected my special rock may have had a part to play in this.

"Do you need to go to the medical room, Arianna?" asked Mrs Battenberg.

"No, I'm fine," I replied, trying to sound casual.

"Let me see your hand," Mrs Battenberg demanded.

When I showed her, she seemed surprised to find nothing wrong and turned her attention back to the rest of the class.

"Sophia, did you see?" I whispered to her.

"Only the blood. Did you cut yourself?" she questioned.

"Yes, badly, but then it healed right back up," I whispered.

Sophia nodded, as though confirming she suspected the Birthstone too.

I smiled to myself. This is exactly what Ethereal said, 'regenerative abilities'. Having these stones might be the most awesome thing ever. I wonder if we could even be invincible!

"I saw you cut yourself," said a voice from the kitchen station in front.

Shocked, I looked up to see Derek. He was the class bully, and he always had to stick his nose in. He regularly tried to get me and my friends in trouble, and he really, really grated on me.

Another thing that annoyed me about him was his rather lazy approach to the school uniform. He did up his tie only loosely; he rolled his sleeves up, and he constantly left his shirt untucked. Personally, I think his uniform was too long for him because he was slightly short and more generously rounded. He required the bigger size. That's why he altered the style, just to try to look *lit*.

Usually he doesn't get away with it as our school is rather strict, but lately I thought the teachers were growing increasingly tired of his persistence and now they just let him off. It was completely unfair.

Or perhaps it was to do with the fact his close uncle, Mr Drayson Black, was the vital connection for getting us into the UK National Space Centre for this year's school trip. Apparently, it was a 'big' thing, because we were the first school to be granted access to its grounds, making troublesome Derek the teachers' current favourite pupil.

"I don't know what you're talking about, Derek," I said, dismissing him in a laughing tone.

"Oh yer? Then why did you wash the blood from your hands? I'm going to watch you more closely, Arianna, and when I have proof that you're a real freak, I'm going to tell everyone," Derek threatened.

Usually, whenever he threatened me, I ignored him and avoided any further confrontation, but this time I couldn't resist. Feeling the anger bubbling inside me, my breathing deepened and my hands tightened into fists as I stared intimidatingly into his smug eyes.

Within seconds, the smugness left his face, the expression quickly being replaced by one of fear. As I stared deeper into his eyes, as though I was searching his soul, his posture immediately straightened. He tried to resist the movement in his arms as they reached up towards his tie, but his arms were completely out of his control. Derek placed his left hand firmly around his loose Windsor knot while his right hand pinched the bottom end of the tie. He gave it one mighty pull, fastening it tighter, then gasped as his eyes widened in shock. Judging from his face, the tie might have been a little tighter than how one would normally wear it.

"Arianna!" Sophia nudged me from my concentration, and I immediately released him from my control.

Derek fell to the ground in complete disarray, his face flushed and sweating. He must have felt highly embarrassed and angry. There wasn't any way he could prove I did anything without risking sounding like a complete loon. Instead, he remained quiet and got back to his cooking.

I returned back to peeling my apples and pondered over what my ability possibly was.

The other girls, Elle, Chloe, Jasmine, and Amelia clearly witnessed what happened with Derek and gave me the thumbs up from the other side of the classroom.

SCHOOL TRIP

Chapter 10

The day finally arrived. As you already know, I'd really been looking forward to visiting the UK National Space Centre. I'd always found the unknown elements of space compelling, and with everything that's happened recently, I felt an even deeper connection to it all now.

Mr Judge informed us the coach journey would be two hours long, but that still didn't dampen my anticipation. I also couldn't help but wonder if there was another reason for the twelve of us going there.

Ethereal could have aligned all this, maybe wanting us to learn something relevant and useful on our trip. Anyway, I would pay close attention to every little thing, seeing if I could find any answers.

The girls and I made sure we were first in line for the coach, so we could rush in and claim the back seats. Then, once we were sitting down, we immediately began unfolding all the strange experiences we'd observed since they'd embedded the stones in us.

"It was so strange. This morning I found myself floating above my bed!" said Amelia, keeping her voice down.

"Well, the other day I caused a bubble-like force field to form around my body when I was being chased by a bee," whispered Elle.

"Guys, I was sitting down for dinner the other evening and had forgotten to lay out the cutlery," added Chloe. "When I went to grab my fork and realised it wasn't there, my index finger merged with my middle finger, transforming into a steel fork! I quickly hid my hand before my parents could notice. I think I may have shapeshifting abilities."

"Oh wow, that's so cool!" said Alicia, glancing down at Chloe's fingers. "Well, I was working on my usual Wednesday night routine of taking apart and rebuilding one of my computers. I noticed a sudden electrical charge running up my arm when I grabbed the power supply. I moved my arm into view and noticed all the laid-out computer parts were moving in sync," she explained.

Ava told us of how she'd first woken up this morning at eight fifty, instantly flushed in the panic of missing our school trip and rushed to get ready. As she was getting dressed, she noticed the rising sun weakening through her bedroom window. It suddenly reversed its course until the night's darkness reappeared. The cars on the road outside were also blurringly moving in reverse. Plagued with the confusion, Ava glanced at her bedside clock once more, which revealed it was now three in the morning.

Zoe was in Spanish class when she was told off by Mrs Lopez for talking whilst she was teaching. Zoe imagined a rather large spider dangling to the left of Mrs Lopez's face, set up perfectly for Mrs Lopez to walk into. The result was Mrs Lopez screaming uncontrollably and frantically shaking her hair as if she'd lost the plot.

"I haven't noticed any powers yet," Malaya said sadly.

"Oh, don't worry, Malaya. I'm sure they'll come soon," Jasmine assured her.

Jasmine accidentally expelled a laser beam from her fingertip whilst trying to dissect her designated lamb's heart in science class.

"Charlotte," said Chloe, "do you remember when you made all of us laugh uncontrollably, out of the blue, in Monday's assembly?"

"Yes." Charlotte laughed. "Sorry for getting us all detention."

The most chilling experience so far was Sophia's. She told us she didn't completely understand it, but she'd experienced some kind of vision of the events of today's school trip and we would soon make a dangerous enemy.

Two seats in front of us sat Derek, who frequently peered over at us throughout the entire two-hour journey. I assumed his suspicion of me must have skyrocketed since our last encounter. I thought I'd better curb my emotions. I couldn't bring any unwanted attention to us right now. We needed to concentrate on getting a hold of all these magnificent powers with no interference. And a full hold, for that matter.

We arrived at the Space Centre at around ten a.m. The building was astounding. They'd designed it to look like the International Space Station, which is orbiting Earth as we speak.

We spent the morning doing team-building exercises, which involved role-playing a mission to Mars. It was so much fun! Then, after a late lunch, we could finally access the dome room, which housed the comfiest cinema-style seats and a 360-degree interactive screen of space—absolutely amazing. The staff ushered us to take our seats in time for the oddly placed drum roll introduction, which seemed to imply a celebrity was about to appear from behind the stage curtain.

When the curtains swiftly parted, they revealed a familiar man.

Yes, that's right, Drayson Black was there. You know, Derek's 'close uncle.' I didn't feel the elaborate entrance was necessary, however. I wouldn't exactly call him a celebrity.

The first thing I noticed was his long white lab coat, accompanied by black accessories from his thick, black-framed glasses to his black chukka boots.

He didn't resemble his nephew Derek in the slightest. In fact, he was the complete opposite. Drayson was tall and frail-looking, with slightly hunched-over shoulders and a pale complexion. I imagined was often cooped up indoors voluntarily, standing behind his oversized telescope, hoping to find the next great discovery.

I wondered if he had any inkling about our orb. The last time I heard him speak, he seemed focused only on the 'asteroid' being sucked up by the black hole hidden behind it. He mentioned nothing about an orb. But then again, maybe he didn't want to let anyone know about it yet. I mean, it would undoubtedly bring loads of unwanted attention from all over the world. Especially from those asteroid mining enthusiasts, who I bet would love to get a hold of our precious orb and start extracting all its priceless crystals, minerals, and metals to sell. According to the news, the compounds believed to have been in that asteroid were enough to start 'the next trillion-pound trading industry'.

Drayson introduced himself. "Good afternoon everyone, and welcome to the National Space Centre. My name is Drayson Black, and you may remember me from my appearance on the news where I was interviewed for my expert advice concerning the recent asteroid threat."

He paused, looking out at the students, as though possibly waiting for applause or at least some kind of acknowledgement. None came.

Drayson then awkwardly clears his throat before continuing. "My research led me to believe that the marvellous asteroid was meant to be our doomsday, the beginning of the end for mankind and all living creation on Earth. But for some strange reason a black hole appeared behind it just in time, saving Earth, saving *us*. I've gone to the trouble of setting up my captured footage taken from my extremely high-tech equipment. I transferred it to display on this magnificent dome screen, so we can all feel as if we were really there. Cool, huh?"

There was no response.

"Now," he continued, "I'm going to play this footage in a slightly slower motion as the black hole begins to absorb the asteroid. This is because, in real time, it happens surprisingly fast."

He pressed play, and the footage appeared on the giant screen above and around us.

"Here we go. See how the asteroid starts to distort as it's beginning to enter the event horizon?"

He paused for a few moments as we watched.

"Within a matter of minutes, the asteroid completely vanishes. Now, did anyone notice something unusual in this clip?"

The whole dome room was silent.

"I'll ask again, did anyone notice something unusual in this clip?" questioned Drayson, in an oddly placed pantomime voice.

It must have been innate because we all instantly responded, "*No!*"

"OK, well let's rewind this clip back to when the black hole starts extracting the asteroid. See just there?" he asked, engrossed in his footage.

Back and forth he played the short clip which revealed an object breaking off from the bottom of the asteroid, positioned just above Earth. The clip also showed the object descending towards our planet.

A sudden sinking feeling filled my stomach, similar to the dreaded feeling you got before going on your first rollercoaster ride. The girls and I looked at each other in shock. My assumption of him knowing about our orb must be correct.

"This object you can see here was aiming to land

on Earth, though I'm afraid the rest of the clip isn't detailed enough to see if it successfully landed on our soil. However, judging from my calculations of its size and density, its success was highly unlikely."

Relief spread across all of our faces.

It must have been obvious as Drayson instantly paused, noticing our reactions. Even though we quickly resumed intrigued, focused expressions, I feared we may have given him enough reason to suspected something.

IN TRAINING

Chapter 11

It was the weekend after the school trip, and it was also the beginning of the last half-term we'd have before the summer holidays began.

And so, the girls and I started meeting up at ten a.m. every day over the half-term; to do our 'power strengthening training.' By the end, we should at least have a vague idea of what powers we'd each come to possess. Seemed the right thing to do, since we didn't get the option of having an accompanying teacher, or even a manual for that matter.

We knew, we couldn't wait around any longer, it was now time to face the responsibilities bestowed upon us and finally try to make sense of it all. Something was coming, we could feel it deep down, within us... something powerful.

All we knew was we'd been given these incredible powers, but we didn't know why. We needed to make sure we knew how to conjure them at will, whenever we needed them.

We met at the usual place: the Stanton shelter. Malaya went to the trouble of researching mythology, and in particular, superhuman mythology. I know, right! Even saying it felt so surreal. Superhuman... me? Crazy!

She laid out everything she'd found but, there wasn't a lot to go on, just pictures of demons, mythical creatures, and folklore. Nothing that resembled us even a bit.

"This is so cool; we're making new history!" exclaimed Ava.

"Quick! We've got to think of a name. What about *Star Girls*?" suggested Amelia.

"Or, how about *The Twelve Stones?*" added Malaya.

"No, no, it needs to be more, well thought out. *Stone-y Chests*!" announced Chloe, laughing a little.

"And you think *that* name is more thought out?" teased Narrisa.

"I've got it! *Astro Girls*!" I announced excitedly.

All the girls widened their eyes as they realised how perfect a fit *Astro Girls* was.

"Great! Now that our name is settled, we're going to have to jump right in and start training," suggested Sophia. "Perhaps we could set up a target and focus our powers towards it?"

We all nodded in agreement. Dangerous or not, we were going for it.

We spent a good few minutes foraging for suitable targets in the field nearby, where our precious orb was resting, and eventually we found a single soda can. This was, by far, the most litter-free field we'd ever seen. We rested the soda can on a nearby rock and took it in turns to focus our energy towards it.

Jasmine was up first. She stood at the marker we'd made from twigs, which we'd placed twelve feet away from the can. As she concentrated, her body faded, and within a second she'd vanished completely. We all gasped in shock, and then a ruby red laser beamed out towards the can, throwing it with great force into the trees behind. A moment later, Jasmine reappeared.

"OMG! That was amazing! I hope my powers are just as awesome," announced an excited Malaya.

Amelia took her place next, standing in position as though she were a goalkeeper about to save the ball, legs shoulder-width apart, knees slightly bent, hands reaching outward. There was even a slight rocking motion within her stance. Noticeably, a luminous turquoise silhouette appeared around the soda can, which then levitated, Amelia controlling its direction with her hands.

"Catch, Elle!" Amelia shouted suddenly, hurling the can towards Elle.

Elle reacted instinctively, a gorgeous blue sapphire aura shining out from her body. The soda can, which hurtled towards Elle froze in mid-air, caged in Elle's force field bubble. Elle then used her powers to place the can calmly back in its resting place.

Alicia was next. As she focused on the can, a surging electrical charge circled beneath her feet, travelling up her body and immersing her entire frame. She was now completely taken over by this electrical charge, which was a stunning amethyst purple. She raised her arm, pointing at the can in front of her, and the amethyst charge ran in a straight line along the ground with lightning-fast speed, connecting Alicia to the soda can. The current was so powerful it started melting the can with its heat. Once Alicia was done, there was nothing more than a metallic, solidified puddle left on the ground.

"Ooh! Let me try something!" Ava announced eagerly.

Ava was so engrossed with her task she didn't even bother to stand at the marker. I watched, unable to see anything significant happening. That was until I glanced over at the metallic puddle and realised the can was reverse melting.

We were all mesmerised by the sight before us; we'd never seen anything like it.

A few moments later, the humble soda can re-emerged in even better condition than before, its previous dents and nicks having all been smoothed out. Even the completely worn-out iconic label reappeared, 'Flitz-lits soda popping beverage'. It was brand new once again.

"Guess it's my go?" asked Chloe.

Standing nervously by the twig marker, Chloe started breathing deeply. Her skin began changing. You could see the cells individually flipping over one by one at a remarkable speed, similar to the effect you'd get from running your finger across a sequined cushion. The shape of her silhouette was altering too, and as we watched, perplexed and amazed, she turned herself into a human-sized pigeon.

Jasmine and Charlotte burst into uncontrollable laughter as Chloe changed herself back.

Charlotte now stepped up, laying the palms of her hands parallel to the ground. Goosebumps consumed her body as an intense expression covered her face, and then a swirling gust of wind appeared from the ground, encasing her completely. Charlotte changed her stance, and suddenly she appeared to be wielding a sword made entirely of her own current emotion and the encasing wind. The aquamarine colouring was hypnotic. She lunged forwards and sliced the can in half, straight down the middle.

"Arianna, it's your go," said Charlotte, before adding, "Ava, you wouldn't mind doing your thing to the can again, would you?"

I walked over to the twig marker as Ava brought the can back to its former glory once again. I was hesitant to perform in front of my friends after all the amazing things they'd done. I didn't want to be laughed at for getting my powers in a muddle. The only experience I seemed to have so far was the incident with Derek back in food tech, and I didn't have much of an audience then.

Anyway, I cleared my thoughts as much as I could and focused on the soda can, trying to replicate the exact feelings I'd experienced back in food tech. Slowly, the can moved, hobbling from side to side as though it was coming to life. As I watched, startled, it travelled vertically down the side of the rock—klink, klink, klink! And then scurried towards the foliage. I focused even harder, telling the can with my mind to come right back and sit down on the rock. I disconnected from my power once the soda can reached the rock. It then dropped lifelessly.

Now Zoe stepped towards the marker, glaring at her target as she did so. The atmosphere was so intense, we could all feel it. A moment later, the soda can levitated to around fifty centimetres above the rock, and then, suddenly, numerous punctures appeared all over the can's surface. You could see the scenery behind it peering through its holes, as though someone got a little too happy with a hole punch!

It was now Malaya's turn. She took her stance and concentrated hard, focusing on the can twelve feet in front of her. Moments passed by and nothing happened.

Malaya looked to the ground in complete disappointment and quietly stepped aside. She was so disheartened that nothing happened; not even a speck of her powers emerged when she'd tried.

"Malaya, don't worry. I bet your power is amazing," I assured her.

"Can't be that amazing if nothing happens," Malaya replied, deflated.

"Right, my turn," insisted Narrisa.

Narrisa had already experienced her healing ability when she accidently healed Alicia, so we all thought it would be interesting to see how her abilities would work in an attack. After all, her healing power could have been one part of her whole power.

Narrisa took her place, closed her eyes, and focused. Her hand rose towards the soda can, her palm open and exposed, and the same golden beam as before came out of her, heading straight towards the can. It appeared she maintained continuous control over the beam, so she focused on her next move. Suddenly, the can transformed—into a can with bat wings!

"Oops," Narrisa responded, slightly embarrassed.

The can shook, its wings flapping madly, and then it flew off.

"Great, now we have no target," said Chloe, frustrated.

"Wow, girls. Check out Sophia!" announced Elle, making us all turn to look.

Unexpectedly, Sophia was engulfed by several holographic hues of oceanic blues. She lifted off the ground, her eyes glazed over and black, and then she spoke in a deep, almost unrecognisable voice, announcing Ethereal's unexpected return.

WARNING

Chapter 12

Fluttering glints of silver appeared above us, hovering in mid-air. To begin with, the intervals were irregular and scattered, but the pace soon quickened as they moved closer towards us. The charge travelled down the atmosphere, touching the ground in front of the resting orb as clouds of mist quickly covered the floor beneath us. As we watched, wide-eyed, the surging currents weakened to reveal a supreme being. She was a glaringly white angelic goddess who possessed most of our human features, but there was something a little… alarming… about her features too. Let's just say if you'd stumbled across this entity whilst on the way home from badminton practice, you'd most likely jump out of your skin, scream to the heavens, and run for your life.

Why would you react in such a way? Well I don't know, it may have been the pair of enormous, iris-less eyes glaring at you, making you feel like you were peering into two identical windows that held the entire universe within them. Or maybe it was the overly long stature, which must have made her an astounding ten feet in height (at least). Her hands were like ours but three times larger, and with far more elongated fingers. She had two arms, two legs, and an extremely long neck, and her skin and hair were, rather peculiarly, the exact colour of freshly churned milk. Ethereal was a superior humanoid.

There seemed to be continuous fog dispelling from her evidently foreign figure, and diamond-like droplets fell from her body, wastefully disintegrating before they could land on the ground.

"It is a pleasure to finally meet you in the flesh, *Astro Girls*," she said, her voice somehow both high-pitched and low at the same time. "Great name choice by the way. I am Ethereal. You have all taken great initiative and pleasingly have come a long way, but your time has been cut short. I'm afraid to say, the Argonauts are now coming for you," she warned.

Cautiously, Jasmine stepped forward. "But they live on the planet Zodiac, which is billions of light years away, right? We won't even still be here by the time they arrive."

Ethereal smirked. "That is correct, but the Argonauts are cunning beings; they will find a way to reach you much sooner."

"Why are they coming for us?" asked Zoe.

"They want what they have always sought," Ethereal explained. "The Birthstones."

"What? We were never told aliens would be after us!" shouted Narrisa.

We all nodded, agreeing with Narrisa's statement, this was horrible news! We weren't ready for the Argonauts to attack us! This is just crazy!

"Ethereal, could you tell us what happened between the Argonauts and Empearions that ended up turning into the great war?" asked Chloe.

"Yes, the Birthstones are rooted deep within the history of the Empearions," Ethereal explained. "The passing of the Birthstones by royal custom of the monarchy has been a traditional practice for many generations, and the ceremonies were constructed beautifully. The Magus, the priestly Birthstone protectors, would be summoned every thousand suns to use their power of purity to remove the Birthstones from the twelve abdicating heirs before placing them within the new ones. However, the last ceremony was sabotaged by the Argonauts, who timed their attack perfectly, appearing when the stones were at their most vulnerable stage—without a vessel. The ambush angered the Empearions, who's provoked rage cast a catastrophic war over the lands of Argon, many innocent beings and creatures were killed throughout Zodiac. The remaining Empearion monarchy was forced into hiding after their old and newly intended heirs were all brutally killed."

"Wow, this is really deep!" expressed Alicia.

Sophia frowned. "So why us? Why did they come all the way here to Earth?"

"There was nowhere for the Birthstones to remain in Zodiac, not enough vessels to reside in." Ethereal told us. "The Birthstones were in grave danger of turning into 'fatal matter.' If that were to ever happen, the entire universe would be irreversibly destroyed. The Birthstones urgently needed new vessels, ones which were as far away from Zodiac as possible, and ones who hadn't witnessed the horrid events. Pure energy had to run through them once more. So, the Magus Priests intervened and sent them to Earth, saving them, saving the universe and also keeping the tradition of the passing of the stones. The reason you were all chosen is because Empearion blood runs through your veins."

"Wait! What? Empearion blood? *Our* veins? No, you've definitely got this all wrong," dismissed Narrisa.

"Please, Ethereal, take these Birthstones out of us!" pleaded Charlotte. "We can't do this. We're only kids!"

The rest of us agreed with Charlotte's plea. No way did we wish to take on this burden, not now we knew we were all in danger. We weren't Empearions. Clearly, we'd got caught up in a horrible mistake. Surely, that's all this was?

"It had to be you, at this untainted age. The Magus saw it, and you cannot question their vision. You are all perfectly capable of accomplishing greatness, and the fate of the entire universe depends on you succeeding."

Ethereal stared at us for a moment.

"The stones carry great advantages; you all have powers and regenerative abilities," she said, as though trying to make us feel better about our situation.

"Ethereal, this must be some horrible mistake," Amelia explained. "There must be someone more suitable than us?"

Ethereal let out a loud, long sigh. "Clearly, the stubbornness of your ancestors also runs through your veins!" She shook her head. "I will explain why you were all chosen."

Narrisa briefly bowed her head in relief before looking to the sky and adding, "Finally, an answer!"

Ethereal paused once hearing her outburst and glanced at Narrisa before continuing.

"You see, there is more to it than you may realise. A few centuries ago, there was a royal Empearion called Iaac. Iaac was next in line to become Tunker, but in his adolescence, he was somewhat rebellious to the royal customs and wished to abdicate his title. Iaac then decided he no longer wished to stay on Zodiac but to instead travel the universe."

No one said a word. We were entranced by her tale.

"He eventually settled and began a new life on Earth, completely cutting himself off from his past life. He showed his love to many Earthian women who, in turn, bore his children. Those children then grew up and had their own children, and so on and so forth, becoming your ancestors. You see? It had to be all of you."

We looked at each other and I imagine my expression reflected theirs. Was Ethereal really saying we had alien DNA?

"Now, you must hold the title bravely, with strength and believe it is meant for you. Zodiac isn't a safe place for the Birthstones any longer, but they still need to reside in Empearion descendants even if the blood is diluted a little. Which is why you have all come to bear them." Ethereal paused for a moment before adding, "Do you all understand now why it had to be you?"

Charlotte opened her mouth to speak but no words formed.

"Yes, we think so… but what does Tunker mean?"

Chloe then stepped into question, puzzled.

"It means 'King'," replied Ethereal.

"King? I can't even process what you've just told us," said Sophia, stunned.

"Well, as you ponder that piece of history," Ethereal continued, "I urgently need to bring you all up to speed. Gobbler!" she cried.

Then the soil rose in front of us until it was peeking above the mist, and before we knew what was happening, twelve huge mounds appeared before us.

"These are common creatures on Zodiac," Ethereal told us quickly. "They are classed as small mammals, though they weigh roughly 190kg. That's about the size of a lion here on Earth. Visually, they resemble your common moles. However, be warned, these Gobblers are vicious and have a nasty bite."

As Ethereal explained the creatures' appearance and composition, the Gobblers appeared entirely from their mounds, staring and snarling at us. Oddly, they did resemble moles, but instead of looking rather timid and cuddly, they seemed ferocious and muscular.

"Attack!" shouted Ethereal.

Her command sent the Gobblers charging towards us with remarkable speed.

My adrenaline immediately kicked in as everything began moving in fast motion. Blinded by the fear, I ran in a panic, soon discovering I was running on my own with a Gobbler chasing me.

At this realisation I jumped and somersaulted backwards, the tip of my toe touching the crown of the Gobbler's head. The Gobbler snorted as it realised I was no longer in its charging path, but was instead above it, hovering in the air.

Then the Gobbler stretched up on its tiny hind legs to make it slightly taller, but its bite was still out of reach. The creature repeated this action several times, and in doing so, I noticed its weakness. Its eyes were clouded over, indicating it probably had poor eyesight.

Behind the Gobbler stood a mature oak tree, and I tried to visualise all its roots becoming exposed and grabbing the Gobbler's feet as though it were a giant octopus attacking its prey. The Gobbler then dug at the earth in a panic, trying to secure itself as my vision became reality. The oversized rodent was no match for the strong, ancient roots bewitched by my powers.

Grab after grab, the multiple roots smothered the Gobbler, clutching the creature and dragging its carcass back beneath the oak tree.

Everyone else managed to stay in the clearing, which made me slightly embarrassed about my immediate flee. The first thing I noticed when I returned was Alicia's virtual electric grip as she stunned her Gobbler into submission. Ava was running super-fast rings around her Gobbler, who ended up spinning into complete exhaustion.

Zoe was inflicting illusional pain on her assigned Gobbler. Elle created a force push attack, which sent her Gobbler catapulting backwards. Narrisa used her magic to overly inflate her Gobbler, restricting it from moving. Jasmine shot out laser beams, which multiplied and expanded until the Gobbler burst open. Charlotte released a sphere full of unbearable emotion, which threw her Gobbler down in agony. Sophia made a crystal ball appear and used it as an orbital weapon, striking the Gobbler dead. Chloe transformed herself into a fellow Gobbler and won her fight, while Amelia used her powers to elevate her Gobbler and then smash it down to the ground.

Rather surprisingly, we all had our Gobblers under control. Well, everyone except for Malaya. She was still struggling, her powers stubbornly refusing to show. She'd put herself out of harm's way, but that meant she was now helplessly stuck up a tree while her Gobbler terrorised her from beneath.

I shouted up to her, "The Gobblers are blind, Malaya!"

I wanted to help her, so I focused my thoughts on creating a slide. It started from where Malaya was standing and ran down the back of the tree, going as far away from the Gobbler as possible. I pictured the slide being made from the bark of the tree.

Malaya noticed the slide as soon as it became visible, her tense posture relaxing at the sight of her rescue. Smiling at me, she quietly removed her jumper and delicately hung each sleeve on some nearby branches so it would trick the Gobbler into thinking she was still there.

Then, slowly, she shuffled backwards towards the roughly assembled wooden slide as though concerned the Gobbler might hear her as she attempted to escape. Despite her fear, Malaya made it safely down, undetected.

"Magical progress, *Astro Girls*. You should be proud," praised Ethereal. "Now, go on your way and rest. You'll need your strength for tomorrow's session."

And with that, she vanished.

HEART TO HEART

Chapter 13

Private Chat between Malaya and me.

Malaya

At 07.00am: "Arianna, are you there?"

Me

At 07:02am: "Hey, you OK?"

Malaya

At 07:03am: "I need to tell you something. Can I come over?"

Me

At 07:05am: "Yer, course you can."

Malaya

At 07:07*am:* "Thank you, I'll get my mum to drop me now."

Malaya was over in a heartbeat.

"Yesterday was crazy. Thank you so much for helping me," she said as soon as we'd sat down.

"You're welcome," I replied. "Just make sure you do the same for me, if I ever need help."

There was an awkward pause for a moment, and I realised I must have said something to upset her. "Malaya, I'm sorry... I didn't..."

"No, it's not your fault, please don't apologise. I just don't know why I'm finding it so hard to use my powers," Malaya admitted, disappointed. "It's so frustrating, you know? I mean, I'm usually good at figuring things out, so why am I finding this so hard?"

I felt so bad for her. I could see it was affecting her, as it would for any one of us if we were in her position. Imagine being the only one unable to use your powers. Especially when she could see us all speeding along nicely, evolving our powers without much effort at all. She was so far behind. And who knew when the threat Ethereal warned us about would arrive?

"Do you still have your scab covering your Birthstone?" I asked, curious.

"Yes, why?" replied Malaya.

"Remember the first time Ethereal came to us all in that dream?" Malaya nodded "And towards the end, she mentioned about the scabs? You know, the part about them healing and as they do, we'll become regenerative? She was right, mine came off just before that food tech accident." I told her, stretching my t-shirt lower to reveal my Birthstone. My flawless oval gem shone so brightly it was almost blinding.

"Oh wow, it's the most beautiful deep green I've ever seen. Do you know what stone it is?" Malaya asked.

"Well, I've done a little research and I think it's an emerald. But maybe this is why your powers aren't working properly yet, maybe you just need to wait until the scab comes off. I can't wait to see what yours will look like," I theorised, attempting to lighten her spirits.

Malaya looked quietly down at her feet.

"Look, why don't we go to the Stanton shelter earlier and get some extra practice in?" I suggested. "It will just be us for a few hours before everyone else shows up, so you won't feel too much pressure."

"Really? That would be great!" Malaya replied, delighted.

We soon arrived at the Stanton shelter. We sat on the bald patch of grass outside the bricked entrance and got straight to work on Malaya's powers.

"OK, tell me what happens when you try and focus on using your powers?" I questioned. "Maybe we can try and work out what's going on."

"Yeah, OK, well, I close my eyes, I try to focus and then, nothing happens at all," Malaya responded in frustration.

"OK, let's try it again together," I said. "Now, I want you to try and clear your mind of any distractions and really focus on your power, visualise the core of it, stemming from your chest."

Malaya took a moment, closing her eyes and breathing deeply. "I can feel something," she announced with excitement, after only a few seconds in.

"Great! Now focus on that energy and try to make it bigger," I encouraged her.

I waited for a few moments but still I couldn't see anything happening.

Malaya broke from her concentration. "Urgh, see! Nothing happens. I don't understand," she cried.

I tried to find words of encouragement, but nothing seemed to surface.

There was another quiet moment while I tried to

think of something else Malaya could try. My attention was abruptly diverted, however, by voices speaking in the distance. They were coming from the next clearing over, where our orb still rested.

"Can you hear that?" I asked Malaya.

"Yes, it's coming from the clearing," she replied with concern.

We crept over to the edge of the bordered trees, remaining camouflaged amongst the healthy green foliage. When we peered over; we couldn't believe what we were seeing.

"Wh... what are you?" Drayson Black asked, terrified.

Why was Drayson Black there, you may ask? Well, I suspected he couldn't let his fascination rest. Ever since he'd retrieved that footage of the asteroid, I bet he'd been on a relentless search to find out where it landed, his suspicion evidently leading him to our precious orb.

It seemed he was extracting samples from it, which raised alarm bells.

However, as he was excavating the samples, he was interrupted by a peculiar activity taking place right in front of him. A giant, garnet red portal stretched open behind the orb, its warped, coloured window making it difficult to see why it appeared in the first place. That was until something emerged from within it.

I tried not to gasp as an unexpected being stepped

out onto the clearing floor.

Thud... thud... thud.

I could feel the powerful trembles of its oddly shaped footsteps as it walked. This being did not resemble us, nor did it resemble Ethereal, not even in the slightest.

The being raised his oddly formed hand, scanned Drayson's body, and then spoke.

"I am Metus, warrior of Argon and dweller of Zodiac," he said. "What is your name, puny Earthman?"

"M-my name is Drayson..." stuttered Drayson Black in shock.

And with good reason. Metus was enormously muscular and extremely tall. His features were distinguished and unnatural looking, which played a big part in his immediately frightening appearance. I could tell he was a warrior, and even a brute.

Similar to a snake's, his eyes were oddly spaced apart, his pupils slit. His teeth were sharp, pointed, and uniform, all of them the same stubby length. His skin was reflective, the colour of the portal consuming his uniquely patterned scales, but his hands were the worst. They were so creepy. There were four fingers, three if you were counting thumbs, although I wouldn't be able to tell you which ones they were. The outer two were a lot smaller than the middle two. His hands also had a natural curve to them, which only served to further emphasise their creepiness.

It wasn't just this 'Metus' here, though; there was another being who stepped out, just after him. This miniature being wasn't even a third of his height and clearly not an Argonaut. He didn't introduce himself. Instead, he fussed and mumbled, prompting Metus with information about our planet. It appeared he was getting this information from some kind of screen projection on his tiny arm. It seemed he was inferior to Metus.

"Earth: 151.05 million km away from its sun. Its life source is thriving. Some may say too much for the human species, but this can be controlled. This planet's minerals are depleting, and harmful waste is increasing to dangerous levels," the unknown alien rambled.

Metus raised the back of his creepy hand and the inferior jumped instantly, stopped his rambling, and was silent.

"Zoobub, I don't have any interest in taking over this pathetic planet. All I want are those Birthstones, and I won't let any puny Earthmen get in my way," Metus informed him angrily.

"Y-y-yes, your Superior Worthiness," stammered Zoobub, bowing down.

"You! Where are the Birthstones?" demanded Metus, pointing at Drayson Black.

"I... I don't know anything about any 'Birthstones,'" replied Drayson, cowering in fright.

Metus grabbed Drayson by the throat, lifting him from his cowered crouch and dangling him effortlessly in the air. "Well, if you don't know where they are then there's no need for your puny life, is there, Earthman?" he asked smugly as he slowly squeezed Drayson Black's throat.

This was too much for Malaya to bear, and she gasped loudly.

I 'shushed' her for fear they'd notice.

"Your Worthiness, something is there, in the trees," alerted Zoobub, jumping up and down.

"Get my gun!" ordered Metus.

Zoobub tottered back and reached inside the portal, and then, with great difficulty, he pulled out a huge alien gun. Malaya and I froze, both of us panicking.

This was mainly because Metus was now pointing the gun towards us, in the direction of the rustling foliage.

Malaya and I made a run for it, and within seconds we could hear Metus pulling on the trigger behind us.

Zz… Zz… ZZAP!

The sounds of electricity shooting from his gun thundered through the trees, coming right up behind us.

I couldn't feel any contact from the weapon, it was a relief to have remained unscathed. My celebratory assurance, however, was short-lived.

I immediately stopped in my tracks as soon as I heard Malaya scream. She'd fallen, caught fully by the gun's ammunition, and was now imprisoned in an enormous net made entirely from electricity, which led back to the Argonaut, Metus.

I cried out for her. "*Malaya!*"

With one mighty tug, they ripped her away from me, and my innate reaction was to run after her. I was, however, too slow. When I reached the clearing, I witnessed Metus walking back through the garnet red portal, dragging his catches with him.

Malaya and Drayson Black disappeared as the portal closed shut behind them.

BREAKING
THE NEWS

Chapter 14

I felt sick. What was I going to tell everyone? What was I going to tell Malaya's parents? Where would I even begin?

Oh, this was all my fault. If I hadn't suggested coming here early, Malaya would still be safe and sound.

I curled up into a ball outside the Stanton shelter and burst into tears as the guilt flooded over me.

As I cried, I awoke a strange and even more exaggerated cry. It was coming from deep within the Stanton shelter.

Stopping my sniffling, I shouted down its descending steps. "Who's down there?"

There was complete silence. Maybe I was hearing things? Or perhaps one of the girls was down there? That idea wouldn't be so far-fetched. I mean, we were meant to be training with Ethereal in half an hour.

I waited a further couple of minutes for a reply, and when there wasn't any, I took a deep breath and ventured down the cold concrete steps.

I made my way slowly, trying to make as little noise as possible, until I reached the final step. I stood there then, my full attention on the darkness before me. It always baffled me, how daylight never seemed to lift the darkness down here.

I could see the vague outlines of our interior furnishings, but as soon as I focused on defining each shape, they would sink back into the darkness once again. It was too dark to see anything. I fumbled for the light switch but when I couldn't find it, I started searching blindly for my new phone to use its light – all while intensely scanning the darkness for any sign of movement.

I suddenly locked eyes with another. These eyes were the most unusual shade of solid metallic grey, and they were located way back into the darkness of the room and low down towards the ground. It definitely wasn't any of the girls, but maybe it was a cat? Or a fox? Or even a badger?

Finally, I got hold of my phone and, shaking, I positioned it towards the peering eyes, turning the torch function on.

"Ahh, please don't hurt me!" screamed the intruder.

I was completely shocked to see what my phone revealed. It wasn't a cat, nor was it a fox, or even a badger. In fact, it wasn't anything earthly at all. It was Zoobub, cowardly hiding in our secret hangout.

Even though he wasn't from Earth, I wasn't afraid of Zoobub at all. I'd already seen how submissive he was. Besides, he was so small and furry.

I could now see Zoobub's features. He was as tiny as I recalled, with shabby teal-coloured fur poking out of what seemed to be an ill-fitting armour-like outfit. It resulted in him having a rather curved shape, similar to a woodlouse. His facial features, however, were comparable to a hedgehog. With his chubby little cheeks, he was admittedly cute looking, but seeing him only fuelled my anger.

"Where's my friend, Malaya?" I demanded.

"Sh-she's now on Zodiac, imprisoned by my Superior Worthiness," replied Zoobub.

"What? She's on Zodiac?" I screeched. "And as a prisoner?" I shook my head in despair. "Wait, why are you still here? And what will he do with her?" I asked, firing off rapid questions.

"I was left behind by mistake," Zoobub sniffed. "I don't know what he will do with your friend, but his Worthiness will not stop," he sniffed again, "until he has acquired all twelve Birthstones," he finished, trying to hold back his tears.

"Why is Metus after the Birthstones? Surely the Magus Priests will just intervene again?" I asked.

"My Worthiness will make sure the ultimate alliance is formed back in Argon, and this time not even the Magus Priests will be able to stop him," stated Zoobub triumphantly.

"And how does he plan on doing that?" I interrogated further.

"Well, he never told me that part," admitted Zoobub, shrugging.

"This doesn't—"

"Arianna, is that you? Who are you talking to down there?" shouted Charlotte as she descended the Stanton shelter stairs.

I don't know why I did it, but I quickly grabbed Zoobub and stuffed him into the wooden ottoman where we kept all our blankets. He was a lot heavier than he looked. "Stay silent," I ordered as I quickly closed the lid.

Charlotte entered the room then, the glaring light coming from her mobile. She scanned the room in search of me. "OMG! What happened here?" she questioned.

Her mortified reaction puzzled me until I glanced at the floor space touched by Charlotte's torchlight. It completely escaped my attention when I was talking to the intruder, but Zoobub had left our usually immaculate hideout in a horribly messy state.

"Elle is so going to freak out when she sees this mess," added Charlotte.

After a moment, Charlotte found what she'd initially been searching for: the Stanton shelter's light switch. The shelter's only source of light was a battery-powered bulb Alicia put down here, back when we'd first furnished the place.

She switched it on, lighting up the whole room to reveal how much of a state Zoobub made. There was all kinds of baffling mess given the few minutes he'd spent down here. He'd already found the blankets as he'd scattered them all over the floor, not to mention the bits of oddly coloured fur he'd left all over the place. There were also puddles of... well, I didn't even want to know what that was! And then there was all of Malaya's research, which was previously pinned to the wall and was now torn to pieces.

However, the most peculiar thing was what Zoobub had drawn on the wall, in place of Malaya's research—an embedded carving of what seemed to be a shrine dedicated to Metus. It was an impressive and intricately detailed portrait of him, something that should have taken at least several days to complete, but Zoobub achieved it in mere minutes. I was, however, slightly distracted by the solitary, stubby candle vertically squished by the side of the portrait. I hoped it wasn't, but it looked like it was made out of earwax. Ew!

"Wow! Did you do that, Arianna? Who's it meant to be?" Charlotte asked, intrigued.

"No, none of this was me," I replied.

"Then who did it?"

I paused for a moment, then cried, "Charlotte, something really terrible has happened."

She frowned, taking a step closer to me.

"What is it, Arianna? Are you OK?" she asked, concerned.

"I'm fine, it's to do with Malaya..."

The rest of the girls arrived then, just in time for me to break the horrid news.

"Wow, what happened in here? Were we burgled?" Sophia asked, raising her eyebrows in surprise.

"I didn't realise we had anything worth taking in here," replied Narrisa, sarcastic as always.

"OMG, OMG, OMG! Try not to step on any germs!" Elle shouted, freaking out.

"Elle, calm down. We'll clean it up." Amelia told her.

"Hold on, we're not all here," noticed Chloe, looking around the shelter. "Anyone know where

Malaya is?"

"I tried contacting her on the way here, but there was no answer," replied Jasmine.

I held my head in my hands for a moment before I stood up straight, psyching myself up for what needed to be said. "OK, girls, I have something serious to tell you," I announced. "You may need to sit down for this."

There was silence as the girls stared at me, waiting for me to continue.

"Early this morning, Malaya contacted me," I carried on, my voice shaking slightly. "She told me how upset she was about not being able to use her powers. I wanted to help her, so I suggested we come here extra early to get some more practice in."

I took a short pause as I tried to summon up the courage needed to explain the toughest part.

"Go on, Arianna," urged Zoe.

I nodded. All the girls looked terrified, and I didn't want to keep them in suspense any longer.

"Well… we must have arrived at the worst possible time. You see, we were practising outside the shelter. Then suddenly, we could hear voices coming from the next clearing over. So, we crept up closer to the tree line to see what the noise was, and it was Drayson Black. At first, he was alone, but then… this enormous Argonaut called Metus emerged from this weird portal. They heard us, and they spotted Malaya. This Metus guy grabbed his weapon and trapped her... and then... well, then they all vanished into the portal. He took Drayson too."

The room was silent for another moment as everyone took in what I'd just told them. Jasmine burst out into tears, and everyone else began to panic.

"Oh no! What are we going to do!" exclaimed Chloe.

"OMG, OMG, OMG!" Elle blurted out in a panic.

"This is really, really bad," stated Charlotte, her glazed over eyes, now puffy and flushed with red.

"So, this is what Ethereal meant by 'we've run out of time.' The Argonauts are here already," clarified Elle, her voice strange and high-pitched.

"And now, they have one of us!" added Zoe, utterly terrified.

"Wait a second... Drayson Black? What on earth was he doing here? Is he in on this?" questioned Sophia.

"It looked like he was taking samples from the Orb... It sounded like he met Metus by coincidence. He was petrified when he saw him," I explained.

Charlotte frowned. "Samples from the Orb? Do you think he knows? About us?"

"That's the thing. I think Drayson was trying to figure things out by studying the samples," I informed them. "You see, Metus demanded that Drayson tell him where the Birthstones were, but Drayson honestly didn't seem to know anything about them."

Ava stood up and began pacing the floor, thinking. "Look," she said after a moment, "we have to do something. We can't just leave her there!"

Ava was right. There was no question we'd have to get her. I wouldn't forgive myself if we didn't bring her back home safely, but how were we even going to get to planet Zodiac without that portal? And, even if we managed to get there, how would we get her back? How would we even know where to look?

That gave me an idea. "There's something else," I told the girls, walking over to the ottoman Alicia and Amelia were sitting on. After asking them to move, I lifted the lid.

They all gasped at the sight of Zoobub.

INTRODUCTION

Chapter 15

Zoobub climbed out of the wooden ottoman, dusting himself off.

"What the heck is that?" shouted Zoe, taking a step back.

"What the heck am I? Like you can talk. Look at all of you! So scrawny and furless. Yuck!" Zoobub replied, insulted.

"Calm down," I said. "Everyone, this is Zoobub. He came through the portal with Metus, but then got left behind."

"What? So, he's the Argonaut's friend?" asked Narrisa in a horrified tone.

"Ha! It would be talliz to consider myself His Worthiness's 'friend'," replied Zoobub, shaking his head.

"Talliz?" I questioned.

"Yes… sorry, a little Huskin crept through there. It means 'stupid' in your Earthian language," Zoobub translated, rather mockingly.

"So, how is it you're able to speak our language?" Amelia questioned.

"My magnificent arm wodge. Its unique Huskin craftsmanship surpasses anything from this planet," Zoobub stated proudly, holding up his arm. "Well, either that, or… it's your Birthstones…" he pondered.

"Huskin? Is that your people, Zoobub?" I asked.

"Yes, my 'people' are called Huskin. We are from Zodiac, and we live in Argon. The Argonauts favour our electronic craftsmanship," Zoobub explained.

"What is it like for the Huskins on Argon?" questioned Charlotte.

"We Huskins are humble creatures. Our historical roots were based in Empeariopia, but as the Empearions saw no use for us, they banished all Huskins from their land."

Jasmine raised her eyebrows. "Banished? Why were you banished?"

"Well, us Huskins like to make full use of the lands

we inhabit," Zoobub explained. "After cultivating too much of Empeariopia, we seemed to have crossed the Empearion values, they see things the opposite way. They believe their kingdom should remain untouched; its beauty unspoilt." He shrugged. "However, luckily for us, the Argonauts shared our cultivation values, so our ancestors made an alliance, agreeing to work on the lands of Argon, and for only the Argonauts. They would receive our craftsmanship in exchange for all Huskins being able to live."

"That doesn't sound like a fair deal; it sounds like you all agreed to be the Argonauts' slaves," Zoe bluntly, pointed out.

"No!" shouted Zoobub rather defensively, before pausing for a moment. "Actually, yes… I guess you'd be right in saying that," he added, realisation blossoming over his face.

Even though Zoobub didn't seem to like us much, there was an innocence to him that made me feel a little sorry for him. These Argonaut bullies seemed to be taking advantage of the Huskins' gifts.

Just then, a familiar stellar voice echoed within our heads. "*Astro Girls!*"

"Oh! We're late for training," announced Alicia. "We need to get to the clearing and tell her what's happened!"

"Zoobub, would you like to come?" I asked.

"No, thank you. I will stay and pray for Metus's

return," he replied, lowering his head.

"Come on, Arianna," urged Jasmine as the other girls left the shelter. "Ethereal might be able to help us with Malaya."

"Wait! Did you just say Ethereal?" Zoobub asked, shocked.

"Yes... why?"

"Oh, my flutterwits!" he exclaimed. "I would be honoured to meet the Almighty Ethereal." He took a bow, then eagerly left the Stanton shelter and made his way to the clearing, Jasmine and I following quickly behind him.

When we got there Ethereal was waiting for us, elegantly hovering in the clearing.

"*Astro Girls,* great forces like yourselves should never be late!" she lectured, pausing when she saw Zoobub. "I see you've brought a friend along with you."

"This is Zoobub. He came from Zodiac and was left behind," I explained.

"It is my humblest pleasure to finally make your acquaintance, Almighty Ethereal," declared Zoobub, bowing low.

Clearly, he'd heard a great deal about Ethereal, and by the looks of it, it was all in the highest of respects.

"It is a pleasure to meet you too, Zoobub," replied Ethereal politely.

"Ethereal," I said, interrupting them, I needed

to explain what was going on, "something bad has happened to Malaya. She's been taken by Metus the Argonaut, who Zoobub was travelling with."

"Yes, I did see that." Ethereal sympathised.

"Really?" remarked Alicia, slightly mystified.

"Yes, I see every event that takes place surrounding the Birthstones," replied Ethereal.

"But then why didn't you stop it?" Raised Jasmine, plagued.

Ethereal sighed, "I know it's impossible to understand at this raw moment. But all this is down to you *Astro Girls*. No one, not even I, can do this for you, we can only help in guiding you."

"Well, can you see Malaya? Can you at least let us know she is OK?" asked Chloe desperately.

"Well, that's where I can do a little better, Chloe; I can show you," Ethereal said.

With that, she drew her long, slender arms outwards and upwards, and as she did, a circular draped curtain rose from the ground. The familiar bewitched veil acted as a screen, projecting a completely devastated landscape, stripped of all its beauty, leaving nothing more than dark soil as far as the eye could see. It must have been Argon.

"You may find the next image you see distressing," Ethereal forewarned, frowning.

The imagery fast-forwarded, and there she was. Our poor Malaya, imprisoned in a barbaric state, crammed into a cage (it was worse than anything I could have imagined). She looked so frightened, so lost.

"Ethereal, can you transport us there? Please?" begged Ava, tearing her gaze away from the projected image to look at her.

"No, I cannot," Ethereal dismissed, "but you *Astro Girls* have the power to reach Argon yourselves."

"But how?" pleaded Amelia.

"Use your Birthstones," Ethereal hinted, her eyes growing shockingly wider.

And just like that, she vanished.

I ran my hand through my hair as I looked at the spot she'd been standing in moments before. It was so frustrating, how we thirsted for her knowledge and how she was so vague in providing it.

"Great, now what?" mumbled Charlotte.

"Well, I guess there'll be no training today," Narrisa said sarcastically.

"We have to find a way to get to Zodiac—and fast," stated Elle, only able to think about rescuing Malaya.

"I could help you get there," offered Zoobub.

"Really? You'll help us?" I asked, pleasantly surprised.

"Of course! I don't want to stay on this horrible planet. Besides, I've seen the powers these Birthstones are capable of, and Ethereal is right. You '*Astro Girls*' can do it. After all, it was Malaya who opened the portal to begin with," explained Zoobub.

"What? She did?" I asked, thinking back to earlier. "Oh, it makes sense now. That's why Metus took her. He knew she carried one of the Birthstones."

"OMG… he must be using her as bait!" realised Charlotte, sickened.

"So what? We're just going to fall into his trap?" asked Narrisa in disbelief. "We're just going to try and rescue her? Do exactly what he wants us to do? *Really?*"

"Well, we can't just not go, Narrisa!" shouted Ava.

Emotions were running high.

"Zoobub, what should we do?" Zoe asked calmly.

He thought for a moment. "Well, according to the Empearion myths, one of you should have the ability to use telepathy. You could possibly use this to communicate with your friend, and—"

"Get her to reopen the portal," interrupted Sophia, as the idea clicked.

"Yes, precisely," replied Zoobub, nodding.

"Well, has anyone experienced any signs of telepathy?" questioned Zoe.

We all shrugged.

"What is telepathy anyway?" voiced Elle, puzzled.

"It's speaking with no mouth," Zoobub, proudly answered, being the only one who seemed to know.

We all looked at him confused.

"Oh, wait a minute, that Earthian definition wasn't

entirely correct. Here we go." Zoobub tapped his arm wodge before correcting himself. "It means speaking to others through your mind."

"Oh! ok, so how do we know which one of us *has* the power of telepathy?" asked Chloe.

"Let's try and find out," suggested Charlotte.

With all of us in agreement, we sat down around the orb, crossing our legs and holding hands as we closed our eyes and tried to focus. We had a theory if we tried to join our energies together, perhaps we would have a stronger connection. Really, we were just winging this whole thing, our imaginations leading us through it all. If this didn't work, we'd keep trying until we made it to Zodiac. Giving up wasn't an option. Malaya needed us.

After a while of sitting there with my eyes still firmly shut; I could feel a bright, powerful beam shining on my face, sending the inside of my eyelids gleaming with the distinctive colour of garnet red. It was the same hue as the portal I'd witnessed earlier with Malaya.

Eagerly, I opened my eyes to confirm what I had assumed. It was there. The garnet red portal had appeared once more. One of the girls had done it. She'd contacted Malaya and had her reopen it.

"Good work!" I exclaimed, grinning.

ZODIAC

Chapter 16

"Yes, it actually worked!" shouted Elle, excited.

"Who managed to speak to Malaya?" I asked, intrigued to know.

"I… I think it was me," said Sophia. "I could hear her talking back to me."

"Well done, Sophia," I praised, the others quickly joining in.

"What did she say? Did she sound OK, Sophia?" Jasmine asked worried for Malaya.

"We will get her back Jasmine," vowed Sophia.

"Yes, Sophia's right, we won't stop until we are all together again," Narrisa said.

As we talked, the portal's presence grew stronger, its liquid currents so hypnotically enticing I wanted to walk straight into it. Instinctively, you would presume something so outlandish and persuasive would scream danger, but it did not. Instead, this tranquil portal seeped a rich humidity into the air, leaving the sweetest taste on your tongue. How did I notice its taste, you may wonder? Well, my mouth was wide open at the time in complete awe of what I was seeing. I knew Malaya's power would be awesome!

"Oh gosh, are we ready to do this?" asked Charlotte nervously as we formed a line in front of the portal.

"I should have brought more anti-bac wipes with me," Elle muttered, focusing (as ever) on the important things in life.

The portal grew wider, now capable of consuming all eleven of us at once (plus a little squeezing room for Zoobub). It was ready to embrace us, but we were lingering, trying to build up the courage to walk into the unknown.

"I don't know why you're all so nervous; the journey will be over in seconds," Zoobub assured us before stepping into the portal and vanishing out of sight.

"Come on, girls, we'll all go together. Just join hands and hold on tight," I instructed them.

"Wait!" shouted Ava. "Do you think we need to hold our breath?"

"Hmm, good point," I said. "Let's hold it just in case."

We all stepped forwards, our hands linked with the firmest grips and our breaths ready to be held. It seemed to be the best way to keep us all safe and together. I mean, we didn't know what situation we'd be stepping into or even how turbulent the journey would be (even if it was only for a few seconds).

When my gripped hand touched the consistency of the garnet red liquid, I shivered a little. The sensation was so surreal. It's hard to explain really, but it felt like we were entering a dense waterfall, one that hosted many powerful and swaying waves compacted tightly into a singular sheet.

Finally, we entered, and the first thing I noticed were the muffled sounds filling my ears. It was like the sensation you'd get from immersing your entire body into a pool of water, the only clear sound being your strong heartbeat pounding away in your chest.

In this brief moment an unsettling feeling came over me, giving me the sense time stood still here. All movements were bewilderingly slower. It was puzzling to me. When Zoobub said the journey would be over in seconds, I'd immediately imagined a lightning-speed passage.

There was an empty space between the portal's

entrance and its exit, which I gauged to be about a foot long. It was connected to what seemed to be a copy of the exact portal entrance we'd gone through. I shuddered as a feeling of 'déjà vu' crept over me. This whole experience was so bizarre and unbelievable to the human eye.

Just as we'd stepped into the portal; our next step took us back out. Our hearing returned, and we took in deep breaths of a thick, almost toxic air. The land we'd arrived on looked exactly like the land Ethereal showed us. With dark black soil placed beneath weird green skies, there were no buildings, no trees, and no visible signs of life. The only familiar thing was the sight of Zoobub. It was hard to miss his teal fur against the darkness of the soil.

"*Astro Girls*, welcome to Zodiac," Zoobub said proudly.

"Oh, it's lovely," Elle replied in politeness, unable to see why Zoobub was so proud of the place.

"Yes, thank you, Zoobub," added Elle, dusting herself off. "Now, how do we get to Malaya?"

"You will have to enter through one of the four faces of Argon," he explained. "Each entrance conjures its own defence against 'trespassers who dare enter it'. Or so the myths say, anyway."

"The myths?" repeated Alicia. "Zoobub, have you ever even travelled *into* Argon before?"

"Of course not!" he shouted. "Huskins aren't

allowed to leave Argon. I was only allowed because His Worthiness requested it. And then what happens? I get left behind!" He started hyperventilating as he remembered Metus abandoned him.

"Calm down, Zoobub," I said gently. "Now, where are these four faces of Argon?"

"Yes, sorry. Each entrance is placed at each cardinal direction," he said in response.

"What the heck does that mean?" asked Ava, glancing at the rest of us to see if we had any idea. I shrugged.

"It means that each one is placed North, East, South, and West," replied Charlotte.

"Wow, how did you know that?" asked Amelia, clearly impressed.

"We learnt about cardinal directions in Geography," Charlotte said. "Don't you remember?"

"You mean you actually listen in class?" asked Amelia, laughing.

"OK, so which one should we take?" asked Chloe, getting us back on track. "Are we closer to any one of the four?"

Zoobub glanced at his arm wodge and informed us we were right in the centre of all four faces.

We thought about possibly splitting up, so we could access all four entrances at once, but we soon decided this would probably be a bad idea. We didn't want to risk losing anyone else; we would be much stronger as a unit. So, we all agreed in travelling to one of the four together, but which one would we take?

There wasn't an obvious choice, especially considering we knew nothing about this planet, its terrain, or any of the surprises that probably lurked beyond its dark soils. It definitely felt like an 'eeny meeny miny moe' moment. A blind pick of the four.

We went with the Southern Face, though there was no particular reason. We all felt comfortable with that choice.

The journey took three long hours, and by the end of it we were all starving and tired of walking on the soil, which was as solid as mounds of dry sand. On that day, the sky above was clear, which offset its freakishly green colour with some light-yellow tones. It felt eerie walking underneath it.

Finally, the soil eased, and a much rockier ground emerged beneath us. We could now see something different other than the usual clear terrain ahead.

Chloe kneeled down, grabbing a fistful of the black soil and letting it escape through her fingers. "We are so far away from home," she said as a tear landed on her closing fist.

NOTUS

Chapter 17

"La… dee… da… dee… daaaah!" sounded a deep, bass voice.

"What on earth was that?" shouted Charlotte as we all jumped.

"Haha, well you're not on Earth any longer, *Astro Girls,*" giggled Zoobub, who hadn't been startled by the voice at all.

"Oh, please don't emphasise that part," begged Chloe, who looked a little green.

"Hmm… hmm… hmmm…" came the bass-like

voice again.

"It's coming from over there!" shouted Elle as she pointed towards the cave-like entrance ahead. We ventured in.

There it stood, bold and impressive. It must have been the entrance to the Southern Face of Argon, burrowed within the dark Argonian soil. Our rocky path connected to its descending cobblestone paving.

Greeting us from the entrance were several decorative archways, rich in unfamiliar carvings that seemed to hold inscriptions of a native language. It must have been Argonian. A bright green light illuminated the writing. It was unclear where it drew its source of power from, but it was obvious the lighting had been placed there for a reason.

Perhaps it was for intruders who stumbled across its undeniably impressive opening? Lighting the way, if they still wished to continue.

"Wow, this entrance is massive," stated Ava as she bent her neck backwards to gaze at the wondrous sight before us.

We wandered around mindlessly until we stumbled across a sealed entrance which, again, had inscriptions written all around it.

"Zoobub, can you tell us what these inscriptions say?" asked Chloe, her thoughts mirroring my own.

Zoobub nodded. "Ahem, yes. It translates to: 'I am—'"

"How dare you!" rumbled the familiar bass-like voice, interrupting him. "Reading my bits as if they're all on display. Oh, wait a minute..." The voice trailed off awkwardly.

"Wow, that scared me!" expressed Elle, a little shaken.

"But where is that voice coming from?" Sophia asked, looking around wildly.

"Hello! Hello! Really? Are you telling me, between all of your twenty-four eyes, none of you can see what's staring right back at you?" replied the voice, utterly amazed.

Slightly alarmed, we all took a step back to analyse every crack and crevice in front of our faces.

"Ah!" we all screamed in terror, jumping out of our skins as we finally noticed where the voice was coming from.

"Ah!" the deep voice replied, failing to replicate the exact high-pitched tone of our screams. "What? What is it?"

"You!" exclaimed Narrisa. "You're... you're a door!"

"Really? Oh! As if I didn't already know that," replied the Southern Face of Argon as it rolled its eyes, clearly unimpressed.

"We didn't mean to offend you. You just really startled us," explained Ava.

"For a moment there, I thought you'd seen a dumbull bat. They're annoying, clingy little creatures.

Ew!" added the Southern Face of Argon before stretching its face out from the door like a turtle would stretch its neck out from its shell. "Ah, that's better. Well, I guess I'd better continue from where you left off," it said, referring to Zoobub. "Ahem, I am the son of the south, the father of the north, the sister of the east, and the brother of the west. My name is Notus and I am the Southern Face of Argon. Be warned, trespassers who dare enter, for your fate will rely solely on your wit," he finished, rather chillingly.

"You know, ever since we've had these Birthstones, things have been a lot more complicated. None of what you just said makes any sense," moaned Alicia, before sighing in frustration.

"Life is about taking journeys and figuring things out as they come," said Notus wisely. "It wouldn't be as much fun if you had all the answers to start with, now, would it?"

Alicia sighed again, folding her arms in disagreement.

"But, as you're clearly not from Argon, I will help a little more by explaining what this passage refers to," Notus continued. "It refers to an old Huskin tale, which tells the story of a father named Borus (north), a sister named Zephia (west), a brother named Euras (east), and a son named Notus (south). They travelled to the four ends of Argon in a greedy attempt to exploit its treasures. These would have made them unbelievably powerful and wealthy, eliminating all their troubles and worries. But as the tale goes on to say, the family failed in their quest and were damned to be punished by an unforgivable force, forever. Their punishment? They were to remain at the four faces of Argon as gatekeepers for all eternity," finished Notus, saddened to reiterate his curse once more.

"Oh, Notus, that's really sad. So, you're stuck here? And like this? Forever?" Chloe replied, unable to bear the thought of Notus's punishment.

"Yes, and for the first few millennia I found it extremely difficult to accept. And you can bet there weren't any dumbull bats around these parts for miles on end because of the continuous crying racket I was making," chuckled Notus.

"You seem to be a lot happier now, Notus," Amelia commented.

"Yes. You would be surprised what time can heal," Notus replied wisely.

"So, what will happen to us if we try and enter the gateway?" questioned Sophia.

"It's difficult to say. The deceptive pathways have their own minds, and I'm pretty sure they've never come across beings like yourselves before," pondered Notus.

"You don't know for sure?" Narrisa questioned.

"I am just the gatekeeper. I decide whether or not you're worthy enough to enter," replied Notus.

"OK, well, are we?" asked Sophia.

"No, definitely not!" Notus said bluntly.

"Oh, how rude! And just what's that supposed to mean?" challenged Narrisa.

Elle then nudged Narrisa before whispering "Don't anger him."

"Why? What is he going to do? He's just a talking door!" dismissed Narrisa.

"Never judge a door by its simple function," lectured Notus. "What I meant to say before, is you most definitely will be attacked. The pathways will likely see you all as a threat," Notus explained.

"So, the only way to enter this gateway and not to be attacked, is being something, the pathways are used to seeing? Like a Huskin or Argonian?" guessed Chloe, as she pondered what the Face was telling us.

"That's right," said Notus.
"But Huskins don't travel in or out of Argon" Zoe rightly pointed out.

"No, but we have always maintained the pathways. I am sure they would know us well," foretold Zoobub.

Chloe then smirked, before suddenly shapeshifting into a furry Huskin, making us all gasp.

"Yes!" exclaimed Jasmine. "Great idea, Chloe. We'll trick the gateway."

"But what about the rest of us?" questioned Elle.

"Wait, I have an idea..." announced Zoe.

She concentrated, and one by one the girls around

me changed into Huskins. I looked down at myself and was disappointed and confused to see I was still the same. Why hadn't she changed me?

Seeing my disappointment, Zoe said, "Arianna, don't worry, I think it's called an illusion projection. I've been practising this power for a while now. *You* can see the real you, but everyone else will see the illusion," she explained.

"Oh, OK," I replied, relieved.

"Flutterwits! Yes, yes! Well done, *Astro Girls*. This should work wonderfully," praised Zoobub as he jumped up and down in excitement.

"Yes, this should do. Welcome to Argon," accepted Notus as he opened up.

We looked at each other, all gave a nod, and then entered through the Southern Face of Argon.

We were now a few steps in, and the illusion seemed to work. There were no attacks, nothing.

It was dim in here, even with the green illumination theme carrying through into the tunnel, oddly placed here and there in every crack and cranny. These green lights weren't a natural part of the tunnel's formation; they must have been as Zoobub mentioned, Huskin-made, like the cobbled walkway that trailed straight through the middle. On either side of the tunnel, its walls were covered in roots. Huge, strong roots that looked as though they'd been there for centuries. I had no idea where the heads to these roots were, as we'd seen there was nothing living on the surface above.

We trekked further in, where it was completely silent. You could hear nothing more than the trickling sounds of water running down the walls and splashing onto the cobbled floor. The dim lighting and water seemed to provide enough nutrients for life to form inside this tunnel, and as we travelled further inside, the foliage grew more and more dense. Different coloured flowers were scattered around, growing from everywhere possible in purples, blues, oranges, and pinks. Every colour you could imagine was visible here. When the cobbled flooring eventually disappeared amongst the continuous growing flowers, we needed to force our way through the shrubs.

Once we pushed through on to the other side of the growth, we noticed a haze of orange light glowing in the distance.

As we edged nearer to a break in the cobbled paving, we stopped in our tracks because we realised there wasn't any more ground left; we were now standing at the edge of a cliff.

"Now, this is my home!" voiced Zoobub as he took in the beautiful scenery.

The impressive views overlooked Argon as far as the eye could see. It was magnificent and even enchanting in its own dark way, the warm orange tones running through the valley and gave it a wicked glow.

"What are those orange lights?" asked Jasmine.

"Those are warning sites," Zoobub explained. "The Argonian soldiers set fires amongst Huskin homes to remind us of how grateful we should be."

"It sounds more like a scaring tactic to keep all you Huskins living in fear," Ava said.

"Are any Huskins ever killed when they do this?" questioned Alicia, horrified.

"Oh yes, every time," Zoobub said quietly. "That's how my family died." His ears dropped empathising his sadness.

"Oh my God, Zoobub!" said Charlotte. "That's so awful... you poor thing."

"How dare they mindlessly kill innocent Huskins like that!" shouted Sophia, outraged.

"Has no one ever tried to stop them?" asked Narrisa.

"No," said Zoobub, "we Huskins are peaceful, honest creatures. We are grateful to the Argonauts for letting our kind live in their land."

Amelia shook her head. "That may be so, but no one should ever have to live in fear like that. It just isn't right."

"How are we going to find Malaya here?" asked Ava, changing the subject as she stared at the valley below. "This place is huge. She could be anywhere."

"Well, she won't be anywhere down there," corrected Zoobub.

"*What?* What do you mean, she won't be anywhere

down there?" yelled an exhausted Charlotte. "We've been travelling for *hours*."

"I hope you're not leading us into a trap, Zoobub," I said, beginning to worry slightly.

"I certainly am not!" Zoobub shot back. "She won't be down there because that is Huskin Valley. She'll be up there. That is where the Argonauts live." He pointed upwards.

We all looked up at the cobblestone sky above this underground valley.

"Zoobub, are you messing with us?" I questioned.

"You *Astro Girls* need to have more trust in Zoobub," he said, glaring at us for a moment before adding, "It has been a long journey. Why don't you all come along with me to Huskin Valley and have something to eat? I will introduce you to a dear friend of mine. Then we can sit down and figure out what our next plan of action will be, over a platter of the finest Nezpits and a cold tankard of drumble-juice," he suggested. He licked his lips in anticipation.

"Mmm... sounds delightful!" Narrisa replied, crossed armed.

HUSKIN VALLEY

Chapter 18

Huskin Valley–what an odd and delightful place. Just imagine an entire underground world full of little busy Huskins, all hard at work. You could feel all the hustle and bustle around you, plus the heat from things being welded. There were clinking, clattering, and slamming sounds coming from the forge, actions that ended with a satisfying hiss of screaming hot metals being dunked into cool water.

After passing the blacksmiths, we moved through the bazaar where all sorts of things were being sold, from strange-looking electrical gadgets to oddly spiked fruit. Well, I only guessed that's what it was when I saw a Huskin take a huge bite out of one as though it was an apple. Must have been a prickly mouthful.

We then walked through many landscapes, from rural farmland to suburban areas, and bridges that passed over green rivers and streams tinted with orange light. After passing the third bridge, we ended up on the outskirts of the busy Huskin town, having arrived at our first destination.

"The Olde Burrows-Bridge Inn," translated Zoobub.

They'd placed the eatery precisely on the dividing line between the city and the countryside, the two opposing lands having a clear division along the ground. You could stand with one foot in the country and the other in the city at the same time.

The inn looked like a charming, cosy, country pub, with a bright yellow, fuzzy thatched roof and colourful rondel glass windows.

Usually, when I go to pubs, it's always on a Sunday, and Mum and Brad always pick ones renowned for their Sunday roasts. Ah, the thought of crisp, herb-buttered roast potatoes, thick gravy, and sticky toffee pudding to finish. The idea took over my mind (and my starving belly), though I guessed that wouldn't be the sort of cuisine available on today's menu. I sighed to myself, I wonder how my family were doing, I hope they are OK and not worrying about me too much.

"OK, *Astro Girls*, it's best if you leave the talking to me," Zoobub told us. "Just nod if anyone asks you anything. We don't want to attract any unwanted attention."

We eagerly took our seats, looking around us and waiting to be served. It was a good thing we had these Huskin disguises; we'd stick out like a sore thumb otherwise.

"I'm so hungry I could 'eat a horse'!" announced Jasmine.

"Me too," agreed Alicia.

"What's a horse?" questioned Zoobub, intrigued.

"It's a big animal. We humans used them in the past to travel on or to work on farms, and these days some humans even have them as pets," Amelia informed him.

Zoobub gasped. "You eat your pet animals?" he questioned in horror.

"No, Zoobub, you've got it all wrong." Ava chuckled. "It's just a 'saying' we have for when we're really hungry," she reassured him.

"Oh, phew. Well, that is a disturbing joke," replied Zoobub, unimpressed.

"Don't you Huskins have any 'sayings' like that?" asked Alicia.

Zoobub thought for a moment. "Yes, here's one. 'I'm so furry, I don't know which end of me is up.'"

"You just made that one up, didn't you?" Narrisa asked, unimpressed.

"Ahem," coughed Zoobub, "no time to answer. Here comes my dear friend Zowena. She's the innkeeper. How do I look?" he asked nervously, patting down his fur.

"Zoobub, you don't 'like' this Zowena, do you?" I teased.

"No! Shh!" he hissed, dismissing me.

Clearly, he was worried Zowena would hear me.

"Welcome to the Olde... Ah, Zoobub, you're back. Where have you been?" Zowena yelled excitedly before hugging Zoobub tightly.

"You wouldn't believe where I've been, Zowena. But I can't say much about it now. I'll have to tell you another time," he replied cautiously as he glanced around the tavern.

"Sure, it's OK, Zoobub. Are your... friends... hungry?" Zowena questioned, playing along.

Narrisa was about to answer, but Chloe used her tiny Huskin foot to press down hard on Narrisa's, reminding her to stay quiet.

"Yes, can we please order a big platter of Nezpits and a whole barrel of drumble-juice?" Zoobub said quickly, his voice raised a little to cover up Narrisa's yelp.

"I'll have it brought to the table right away," assured Zowena, before walking back to the bar.

"Oops, sorry," apologised Narrisa.

"Narrisa, are you feeling alright? It's not like you to apologise," teased Alicia.

"Here you are. Your jumbo platter of Nezpits and a whole barrel of drumble-juice."

Zowena had appeared back at the table with our order in record time, smiling widely.

"You must all be really thirsty. Let me know if you need anything else." With that she winked, giggled, and walked off.

Zoobub watched her go, sighing. "Doesn't she have the most blubberful giggle?" he said, mesmerised.

We couldn't help but laugh at Zoobub's obvious fondness for Zowena.

I glanced over at the platter Zoobub ordered. Oh, how can I even begin to describe the sight of these Nezpits? Basically, what Zowena had given us looked like a platter filled with lots of different kinds of deep fried, shrivelled insects. And the smell... Well, the smell wasn't too bad; it strangely reminded me of cheeseburgers and grilled onions. However, the girls and I'd already made our minds up to pass on the Nezpits, unlike Zoobub, who was elbow deep in his end of the platter within seconds, happily crunching away.

It was then I noticed the garnish around the platter. It vaguely resembled bread, and it looked pretty tasty. At least, I hoped it was bread. "Zoobub, what is that around the Nezpits?" I asked.

"Ah, that's called 'Crot'," he explained. "It's just to

make the platter look fancy. Huskins don't eat it, but you can try it if you want."

I picked up a clump of Crot and tore a few pieces off, sharing it amongst us *Astro Girls*, all of us hoping it was delicious, wholesome bread. We all took a bite and, pleasantly surprised by the taste, we scoffed the lot. Zoobub had to order a lot more of this 'Crot', which raised suspicion amongst the punters.

Charlotte then turned the tap on the barrel of the drumble-juice and waited for the juice to come out. "I think its empty, Zoobub," she said.

"No, it's full, it just needs a minute or two to make its way down," replied Zoobub, his mouth full of half-chewed Nezpits.

Just as Zoobub said, the cold, purple gloop finally made its way down into the crystal tankard. It didn't look like any juice we knew of. It was more like a mixed berry milkshake, with fancy flecks of glitter in it. Mmm...

We all looked at each other, wanting to take our first brave gulps together.

Three... two... one... and down the hatch it went. The consistency was unbelievably thick; we had to swish it back and forth between our teeth to make it runny enough to swallow.

Oddly, though, it was yummy, and it tasted like a fruity milkshake. We quickly polished off the whole barrel.

Zoobub was staring at us, astonished. "I'm surprised you like drumble-juice so much," he said. "Some Huskins can't get over what it's made out of—"

"No, please don't tell us," Ava begged him, rubbing her full belly.

"As you wish," replied Zoobub, nodding. "Now, about getting to Malaya. Can you see the line running between the city and the countryside?" he asked, pointing out the window.

We nodded.

"Well, half a day's walk down that line is a tower called 'Valdome'. This dominant black tower was ordered by the Argonauts to be built as a protective measure against the Empearions, and to this day it is patrolled by Huskin guards. You see, they were worried the Empearions would be plotting their revenge after their ceremony was brutally ambushed by the Argonauts. The Argonauts are aware of the Empearions' strengths," Zoobub explained. "They are patient, calm, and calculated, whereas the Argonauts are brutal, powerful, and reckless."

"Well, I don't know how the Empearions can stay so calm. If it were me, they'd all be finished by now," declared Narrisa.

"Make no mistake, the Empearions will have their revenge, and the Argonauts know this," Zoobub assured us.

"OK, so how do we get through the guards?"

questioned Jasmine.

"It will be tricky," Zoobub warned us. "The tower is heavily guarded. *Astro Girls*, this will be the last obstacle between you and Metus. There will be no turning back and definitely no second chances so use those powers wisely."

"The power part isn't going to be easy," Sophia said, sounding worried. "We still don't really know what powers we actually have."

"This is true," said Zoobub, thinking for a moment. "I have an idea. Follow me." With that, he tipped the enormous platter of remaining Nezpits down his little throat before making his way over to the bar to thank Zowena.

"I must warn you," Zowena whispered into Zoobub's round ear, "I overheard one of the punters saying, as they were leaving, that they were going to inform the local Argonaut guards you were here. Apparently, they're searching for you. It didn't sound good at all."

"Don't worry, Zowena, we'll be long gone before they can reach us," Zoobub reassured her before kissing her furry forehead.

"Aww!" we all cooed when we saw what he'd done.

Zoobub turned and frowned at us, highly unimpressed.

"Come on," he said gruffly. "Time to go."

So off we went, ready for our next stop.

TARN TORMENT

Chapter 19

We were on the move once again with no clue what our next destination would look like.

At first, I thought we might have been making our way over to Valdome Tower, but we were no longer travelling on the dividing line. Instead, we'd crossed over, entering the countryside, which was as beautiful as the countryside back on Earth. However, being on Zodiac, there were some differences. Maybe it was the way the blue grass was moving in the breeze? A quick glance at it and you would have been fooled into thinking it was a flowing lake. Or perhaps it was the blue trees? With their white branches moving up and down with every inhale and exhale, they seemed as though they were truly alive. I glanced around, looking for any clue where we may be going, but I couldn't see anything other than the rolling hills that backed onto the sharp, uninviting mountains.

"*Astro Girls*, be careful of the dark creatures that lurk in these lands," warned Zoobub.

"Oh, we can handle them, just like we handled those Gobblers," Narrisa replied smugly.

"Ha, Zodiac is home to far scarier and far more mischievous creatures than Gobblers," Zoobub assured us.

"Mischievous? What creatures do you have here that are mischievous?" asked Ava, intrigued.

"The Imps! They are the most mischievous creatures of all."

"What makes them so mischievous, Zoobub?" asked Chloe.

"Because they are erratic tiny pests that impulsively tease, prank, and lead you astray if you give them the chance."

"They sound annoying," Chloe commented.

"Yes, they are," agreed Zoobub, "but make no mistake, they are devious and likely to cause despair. You'll be lucky if you don't have to cross one."

"Zoobub, where are we going anyway?" asked

Amelia.

"I thought it would be a good idea for you all to see the Magus Priests before trying to rescue Malaya," explained Zoobub.

"That's a great idea," I replied, relieved.

"Why is that a great idea?" Ava asked, turning to look at me.

"Because they're the ones who sent the Birthstones to us in the first place. Don't you remember the story Ethereal told us?"

"But aren't we wasting time? What about Malaya?" asked Jasmine, worried about our friend.

"Look, we could try and go to Valdome Tower now, but we can't make full use of our powers," I told them, "which means we'd most likely get captured, just like Malaya. If that happened, then the Argonauts would finally have what they want—our Birthstones—killing us all just like they did with the Empearion heirs."

We all agreed it was too risky. If the Argonauts captured us all, then it would definitely be game over. Malaya was safer alone than with us trying to rescue her without a real plan.

We continued walking over the hills, and after climbing the final one, Charlotte brought our attention to some strange red mist in the distance. It seemed to be a swaying swarm of some kind.

"Zoobub, what is that?" Charlotte questioned.

"Oh no! Remember the imps we spoke of? Well,

that's them," Zoobub told us.

"Great," groaned Amelia. "How are we going to pass? They're literally everywhere."

"We're just going to have to pass through," Zoobub stated, taking a deep breath as he prepared himself for the task ahead. "Remember, they are tricky little imps; they will try and lead you astray."

Cautiously, we made our way through the red mist.

The imps were creepy little things. They were the size of my hand, and they had entirely blacked-out almond-shaped eyes, red skin, and bony, bat-like wings. They also had two stubby gold horns resting between their long, pointy ears, which flopped over and hung behind their head, stopping halfway between their wings. Underneath their flopped ears they all had shiny, curly, golden spun hair.

They knew we were there; they took it in turns to pause and give us an eerie look before whizzing around us, only to pause once more and give us the same eerie look all over again.

"Oh gosh, they're watching our every move, plotting against us," whispered a panicked Elle as she cautiously stepped through.

Suddenly they all stopped whizzing around and froze on the spot, like little statues.

"Wh-what's happening?" Jasmine asked, unnerved by their movement, or lack thereof.

Narrisa stepped closer to one imp, peering down at

its eyes as it continued to hold its frozen stance.

Apparently, the imp could no longer hold its eyes open as it twitched to blink. Then, clearly angered at having been caught out of their own playing dead game, they un-paused. In a second, they'd all turned nasty and vicious, jumping up and attacking us all.

"Argh, they're scratching me with their claws!" screamed Ava.

"Me too!" seconded Sophia.

"Oh, I just remembered something. 'If an imp should ever attack, a golden thread will counteract'," said Zoobub, remembering an old Huskin rhyme.

"What does that mean?" shouted Chloe as she kicked one imp off her.

"I was never really sure," admitted Zoobub.

"It's... it's their hair!" shouted Alicia in excitement as she revealed the hidden clue.

"Oh yes, of course," replied Zoobub, astonished he'd missed this obvious clue in all his years. "All of you, pull a single thread from their heads," he instructed.

We all grabbed a hold of our imps and plucked a single shiny golden thread from the back of their heads. As soon we plucked the threads, the imps vanished. The rest of the imp crowd then dispersed abruptly, making us sigh with relief. At least now we knew their weakness.

"Phew, that was becoming increasingly annoying,"

sighed Jasmine.

"I'm glad you remembered that rhyme, Zoobub," I said. "Thanks."

Now there was no red mist covering the landscape, we could see we'd reached the bottom of the mountains. At its base lay a rich purple pool, which was where Zoobub stopped.

"Why have we stopped?" wondered Amelia aloud.

"Because we're here. And we made it with only one interruption," boasted Zoobub. "The creatures here must be able to sense that you all bear the Birthstones."

"Well, that's a relief, but where are we exactly?" asked Chloe, peering down at the pool.

"At Tarn Torment, of course! Now, one of you will have to dip a part of your body into the water to open it," Zoobub explained.

"Yeah, right. I won't be doing that," said Narrisa dismissively.

"I'll do it," volunteered Elle.

"Really? Are you sure, Elle?" Narrisa asked, astonished. "Aren't you afraid of the germs that could be in there?"

Elle removed her shoes so she could dip her toe into the purple water. I guess she thought was the furthest part away from her face, and so was less likely to get infected. As brave Elle dipped her toe in, the colour of the water changed, transforming from a rich purple to an inviting, rippling pink.

"Great! Tarn Torment greets you. You can now enter," said Zoobub.

"Tarn Torment doesn't sound friendly," Ava pointed out.

"Well, it isn't meant to," replied Zoobub. "It's called Tarn Torment because its waters test the strength and sanity of those brave enough to enter it."

"I'm sensing a theme here," Narrisa commented.

"Er, so why are we entering it, Zoobub?" asked Jasmine, bewildered.

"Because this is the only way to the Magus Priests. Oh, and don't worry," said Zoobub quickly, "It's also said that the only ones who *should* enter are the chosen Birthstone bearers. So, you should all be OK."

"Strength and sanity? Oh Narrisa, you'd better sit this one out then," teased Sophia, grinning.

"Ha-ha," replied Narrisa as she wrinkled up her nose, unimpressed.

"Now, even though I am 98.9% sure… no, wait… 99.9% sure that you will all pass through unharmed," said Zoobub. "You should know about the grave warning of Tarn Torment. There is even a remembrance song, which tells the story of the young Huskinling who didn't listen to the olden tarn's tale and was doomed to wander the uninhabitable plane for all eternity. It goes like this."

Yelped, Huskinling. Oh, Huskinling.
To eyes' you have not awakened.
Your br-av-ery has betrayed yo-u.

Yelped, Huskinling. Oh, Huskinling.
You will forever lay in tor-ment.
For the purple tarn has not greeted you.
Your sanity has now left you.

When Zoobub finished singing, he said, "The Huskinling thought he could trick the Tarn into accepting him, but the Tarn only accepts the *truly* chosen. Now, the tale speaks of the Huskinling wandering the Tarn, waiting to inflict his eternal pain on any others who dare enter, in the hope that the Tarn will release him. Remember, you must all follow and focus on the neon spiral fish," he finished. "This is important."

"Zoobub, you're prepping us as if you're not coming," gulped Amelia.

"Yes, your suspicion is true. I'm not coming," Zoobub admitted. "It would have been nice to see for myself if the legends of the Magus Priests' home are true, but I'll just have to wait and hear it from your lips later. Without a stone, I'm not eligible to enter," he sniffed.

"Oh, I really wanted you to come, Zoobub," said Charlotte, sadly.

Zoobub smiled at us.

"OK, are we holding our breath again or what?" asked Narrisa as she stared at the water.

"You can if it makes you feel better, but as you're the Birthstone bearers, you'll be able to breathe under this water without any problems," Zoobub told us.

"OK," said Alicia, biting her lip.

As we plunged ourselves into the tepid pink water, the neon fish appeared from beneath, circling around us before starting to light our way, deep beneath the surface. We gazed at them for a moment before deciding it was time to dive in completely, and I could feel the bubbles passing by my limbs as I descended.

I looked at my watery surroundings. I couldn't see any landscape around us, nor any floor below; there didn't seem to be an end to this strange pink tarn. I guessed that was partly why Zoobub expressed the importance of these neon fish, to prevent us from losing our way or succumbing to the tarn, like in the tale.

I must keep my focus on these fish, I reminded myself.

They looked so elegant with their skirt-like fins dancing in the water's stillness, swirling around their bodies in a continuous spiralling loop. It was clear to see how they got their name 'spiral fish.'

We'd now been under the water for over a minute and the struggle to breathe was becoming overpowering. Charlotte, Amelia, and Ava were the first to cave in; they grabbed their throats as the strange transitional feeling from air to water began flowing through their lungs, and inevitably, the rest of us followed.

Once my body resumed its harmonious functions, I focused back on the spiral fish. Many more appeared, swarming together to form a twister-like tunnel, their neon colours reverberating through the inside of the vortex.

The internal view reminded me of those optical illusion wheels, calmly spinning as they grabbed your full attention. And it became immediately apparent why the distraction was here; something was happening to the pink waters surrounding us. The temperature was rising, and soon enough, the source came into view. It was an enormous face, so gigantic the vortex was the perfect size to be its nose. This taunting face stretched its mouth wide open. At the sight of its large gape, I instantly felt a great weakness in both of my knees, not to mention a powerful sinking feeling deep in the pit of my stomach.

I remembered what Zoobub said about the spiral fish being important, so I focused on them again, trying to ignore the haunting of this Huskinling as we rushed into the vortex.

It was safe in here; I could feel a kind of tranquil hypnosis coming from the school of spiral fish. The water returned to a comforting, lukewarm temperature, and we happily swam through until we reached the end. I could feel the pressure building under us as we swam deeper, pushing us up and up until we were all forcefully propelled out of the tarn.

THE MAGUS

Chapter 20

We landed on a cold white marble floor, which was full of tiny, shimmering gold flecks. The walls and ceilings were encrusted with white crystals, and the entire space was well-lit, making it sparkle and glisten beautifully. It felt like we were standing within a giant geode rock, which then reminded me of the inside of our orb. There was something so heavenly about the cave we'd ventured into; I immediately felt calm.

Standing in front of us were three beings, their appearance different to any other beings we'd come across so far. Their faces were long and gaunt-looking, and their eyes housed horizontal pupils, similar to those of a goat. Their strange noses held no structure; all that was visible were two nasal passages located halfway down their long, rectangular faces. The texture of their skin seemed human-like, but with enlarged skin cells, which contained an unusual blueish-purple pigment. The palms of their two-fingered hands were a pale pink, as were the centres of their faces.

They all wore long white formal robes, beautifully bordered in shimmering gold.

"What is this?" one of them cried. "Huskins have invaded our legendary cave. You're either brave or stupid to be here. Either way, regret will linger in your remaining essence once I have finished with you."

This being seemed to be the leader of the three as the other two didn't speak. We stood there in shocked silence as the leader raised his hand, conducting a powerful surge of energy. It seemed this being was ready to strike us all.

"Wait!" shouted one of the other beings. "Korsal, look!"

"What is it, Gaelic? How many times must I tell you not to interrupt me when I am casting," replied Korsal angrily.

"Their chests! They carry the Birthstones!" shouted Gaelic.

"Oh, why yes! They do!" admitted Korsal. "That

would have been rather embarrassing."

Zoe removed her illusion projection from us then, revealing our true selves.

"Ah, welcome to our home, *Astro Girls*," said the leader with a smile. "It is a pleasure to finally meet you. My name is Korsal, I am the Elder Magus. This is Gaelic, and this is Larso."

"We absolutely applaud you on your impressive strength so far. How are you getting on with your Birthstones?" asked Gaelic.

"Thank you for not striking us," Amelia blurted out. "This is all overwhelming to us. We haven't experienced anything of this nature before," she explained.

Narrisa stepped forward. "We're finding the Birthstones challenging too; we weren't exactly shown how to use them," she said in a slightly sassy tone.

Chloe nudged Narrisa with her elbow, glaring at her to stop talking.

"Er, yes..." mumbled Gaelic. "Unfortunately, the power within these Birthstones can't be taught through usual means, and in so little time. Usually, the amalgamating journey between birthstone and bearer; takes... well, at least half an Earthian century. But even so, you have all been taken on many adventures, which you must have thought were only possible in your wildest dreams. It is a lot to take in," he added, reassuring us.

"So, what brings you to our glorious home?" asked Larso.

"One of us was taken captive by the Argonaut, Metus. We're here to seek your help," I responded.

"Your friend, Malaya," answered Korsal, nodding.

"Yes. How did you know?" asked Ava. "Anyway, we need to enter Valdome Tower, where she's been imprisoned."

"Yes, of course," said Korsal slowly, "but first I must ask, are you aware of the risks if you should all fail in rescuing Malaya?"

"And are you aware that Metus is using Malaya as bait to capture you all?" added Larso.

"Yes, we are, but we can't just leave her there to be killed," Jasmine pointed out, before continuing. "Would you not save her if you were in our position?"

Both Gaelic and Larso grasped Jasmine's hypothetical question.

"We cannot comment on such trivia. Our sole part in this is to choose and place the Birthstones into the bearers. After that, it is your joint responsibility to keep each other safe. Now, what to educate you on first..." wondered Korsal as he tapped his finger on his chin.

"Oh, oh! Let's tell them about their individual powers!" enthusiastically suggested Gaelic, clapping.

"Yes, a great suggestion," agreed Korsal.

We all waited with bated breath.

"Amelia," prompted Korsal.

Amelia straightened her back with the abrupt calling of her name. Korsal then began pacing the floor with his arms folded behind him.

"You carry a turquoise Birthstone. This is because you are an Aquarius. This means your power ability is Telekinesis Levitation. Simply put, you can move desired objects with your mind."

Amelia's eyes darted around as if she were processing the information.

Korsal then stopped pacing and without waiting for Amelia's reply, he swiftly called out the next name.

"Sophia, you carry an opal Birthstone because you are a Libra. This means your power ability is Clairvoyant Telepathy. You can see the future within the present and speak to others via your mind," continued Korsal.

Relief seemed to have blossomed over Sophia's face.

"Chloe."

Chloe began stroking her agate Birthstone with reassurance.

"You carry the agate Birthstone as you are a Gemini. This means your power is Shapeshifting. You can change into any object or living organism as you desire, and also use its powers should you choose."

Her eyes widened as Korsal's words sank in.

"Alicia, you carry the amethyst Birthstone as you are a Sagittarius. This means your power ability is

Technopathy. Simply put, this means you can control electrical components with your mind and use their electrical charge at will."

Alicia displayed the biggest smile while fist-pumping the air.

"Ava, you carry the peridot Birthstone because you're a Leo. Your power ability is time travel. You are able to move back and forth in time. This ability also lets you move at lightning speed."

Ava's eyes widened in shock as lighting speed was mentioned.

"Zoe, you carry a diamond Birthstone because you're an Aries."

Zoe kept her gaze, nodding in agreement.

"This means your power ability is Psychosomatic Illusion. You are able to cast powerful illusions, capable of causing trauma and having physical effects on your chosen targets."

"I knew it was a diamond!" Zoe jumped in excitement.

"Arianna, as a Taurus, you carry the emerald Birthstone, which means your power ability is Body Control. This means you're able to control the actions of your chosen targets, and you can also give non-living objects minds to control."

I felt a flutter in my belly. It was such a relief to finally know what my powers were and the more trivial thing of having confirmation that my Birthstone was, in fact, emerald.

"Elle, as a Virgo you carry a sapphire Birthstone, which means your power ability is Force Field. Simply put, you have the ability to create protective bubble force fields around yourself and any chosen targets, and you can also send a force to push and pull objects or beings."

Elle nodded in acceptance.

"Narrisa, you carry an imperial topaz Birthstone, and this is because you're a Scorpio. Your power ability is Sorceress. You are able to heal and cast spells at will."

"Wow…" Narrisa was in shock.

I mean, we all knew she had the healing part, but a sorceress? We all gasped.

"Jasmine, you carry the ruby Birthstone because you're a Cancer. This means your power ability is Light Manipulation. You are able to bend light to your advantage. You can cast laser beams, and you can also turn invisible."

Jasmine tapped her fingertips together in excitement.

"Charlotte, as a Pisces your carry the aquamarine Birthstone, meaning your power ability is Emotion Manipulation. This means you have the ability to control the emotions of your targets."

Charlotte raked up the hair from the side of her temple before scratching it, her gaze, clouded.

Korsal paused whilst Gaelic and Larso turned away

for a moment. When they turned back, they held a little red box between them.

Korsal continued. "And finally, there is Malaya. Malaya is a Capricorn, and she carries the garnet Birthstone. Her power ability is Teleportation. Simply put, she is able to create portals to any desired destination."

We all held onto each other in support.

"I hope this clears up most questions you may have about your individual powers," Korsal said. "There is something else, however. Together you all have additional powers. As well as being able to fly, you are also able to manipulate your birth sign elements – fire, water, air, and earth – which is the fashion theme of my next task."

We exchanged nervous glances. What on earth was he going on about now?

"Now," Larso instructed, "I will need three of you at a time. Can I have the air signs first, please? That would be Narrisa, Jasmine, and Charlotte. I will need you all to stand on this engraved circle here."

Without saying a word, Narrisa, Jasmine, and Charlotte took their places within the gold circle on the floor.

"Eck-too aloo hava," announced Larso.

The circle expelled an upward gust, swivelling out bright hues of white and yellow, which hazed over the three chosen girls, barricading them within. As the

169

rest of us watched, their clothing started morphing into something totally different, and when the gust weakened it revealed Narrisa, Jasmine, and Charlotte in their glorious new attire.

The white and yellow theme ran through all three of them. However, each individual outfit was unique, the colours of their individual Birthstones predominantly running through their clothes, eyes, and hair. Narrisa's eyes and hair were now a gorgeous amber, Jasmine's were a vivid ruby red, and Charlotte's were a light aquamarine blue. An intricate gold pattern framed their Birthstones, leaving the gems uncovered and shining in all their bewildering glory.

"Now I want the fire signs," said Larso. "Zoe, Ava, and Alicia."

The requested three changed positions with the air sign girls. Now, all the fire element girls were standing within the engraved circle, ready for Larso.

"Eck-too aloo aga," he sang.

The same gust appeared once again, encasing Zoe, Ava, and Alicia, but this time the hues were orange and red. When the swirling gust weakened, the girls appeared in their new custom outfits, which carried the same orange and red theme. Zoe's hair and eyes were now a greyish white, Ava's were now a bright green, and Alicia's were a lovely deep purple.

"Now, the earth signs... Arianna, Elle, and Malaya," requested Larso.

"But... Malaya isn't here," I pointed out. "Will she still receive her outfit?"

"Yes," Larso replied, annoyed at being interrupted. "I will explain in a moment. Now, please step into the circle so I can finish my masterpiece."

Elle and I stepped inside the circle.

"Eck-too aloo dharati!" he shouted.

The gust appeared around me, Elle, and the little red box, which Gaelic and Larso placed beside us. Our side of the gust was reflective; as though it were a mirror. We could see ourselves changing, transforming from the old, normal girls we knew to the new exceptional supergirls we'd become. Our outfits were beginning to appear, similar to the other girls', but our themed colours were green and brown. Elle's eyes and hair were now a vivid sapphire blue, while mine were a deep, earthy, emerald green.

"Now, the remaining water signs... Amelia, Sophia, and Chloe. Enter the circle," demanded Larso, eager to finish.

We changed our positions with the water element girls, and when all three of them had taken their stances, Larso announced, "Eck-too aloo pani."

The swirling gust appeared once more, this time in hues of blues and greens. The girls came into view once again as the gust finally weakened, revealing outfit themes of blue and green. Amelia's eyes and hair were now a beautiful turquoise, Sophia's were a milky white speckled with different holographic colours, and Chloe's were a warm yellow.

"Now," said Larso, once we'd all been transformed, "this little red box is meant for Malaya. Make sure it's given to her the moment you are able to."

"You all look stupendous," announced Gaelic, excited.

"*Astro Girls*, your transformation is complete," Korsal said happily. "You must now be on your way to Valdome Tower. So, let's give you all a head start."

With that, he started chanting, "Zah zomere kartu! Zah zomere kartu! Zah zomere kartu!"

VALDOME TOWER

Chapter 21

With a blink of an eye we were no longer with the Magus Priests, nor were we inside their remote cave. Instead, Korsal had transported us right in front of Valdome Tower.

As we stared up at the ominous structure, it quickly became apparent this wasn't just a tower. This was a mighty dark fortress. Its unreachable walls were encased with deadly sharp, black steel planks, and they finished the whole thing off with an array of uninviting defences.

What made it even more menacing was the fact we couldn't even see the top of this giant tower as it looked like it rose beyond the cobblestone sky.

"Oh! Hehe! Gibbering outfits, *Astro Girls*!" shouted Zoobub, jumping up and down in excitement.

"Zoobub!" cried Alicia, pleasantly surprised. "I'm so glad the Magus Priests didn't forget to transport you too."

Zoobub grinned, still jumping up and down.

"You know, I can't stop running my hands up and down this fabric," said Elle, ignoring the tower as she checked out her new lightly armoured outfit. "I haven't felt anything quite like it before."

"I know, it's amazing how perfectly they fit," Amelia agreed. "They're definitely one of a kind."

"How was it?" asked Zoobub eagerly. "The home of the Magus Priests? I want to know every little detail."

Zz... Zz... ZZAP!

A sound I found both chillingly familiar and utterly horrifying abruptly interrupted us. It was coming from the concealed entrance of the tower.

Zz... Zz... ZZAP!

Another continuous electrical beam fired towards us, and this time Alicia lifted her arms to attract the scattered electrical charge. It enveloped her entirely; the electrical surge silhouetted her body. I saw how effortlessly she controlled it, and I felt a proud tingling sensation rushing through me giving me goosebumps. I mean, she looked so cool. We *all* looked so cool!

Alicia then levitated off the ground, pushing the electrical charge away from her and back to the concealed entrance of the tower. It was as though she'd caught a boomerang and thrown it straight back. The action was seamless, just like a pro.

As we stood there in front of the tower, it seemed clear to me that visiting the Magus Priests had definitely been worth every second. We didn't just look different now; we *felt* different. More in control and more confident in our abilities. It must have been down to finally knowing exactly what each of our powers were.

The entrance was now visible, the impact Alicia made having burst it open. We knew what we needed to do: reach the top of the tower, enter the Argonauts' lair, and finally save our dear Malaya. I wondered how she was doing, our poor, sweet Malaya.

With that thought in mind, we moved forwards, filled with enough vengeance to enter this tower and stop anything that tried to harm us on our way up.

But first, we needed to get inside.

As soon as we moved forward, huge, lethal-looking spikes rose from beneath the shaking ground, right under our feet.

Elle reacted instinctively, creating a bubble-like force field to protect us from all the threats around us and partially, at this moment, the sharp ones below.

"Girls, don't move!" she shouted at us.

As we stood, frozen to the spot, the big spikes pushed the force field upwards, causing us to travel up a good few levels of the tower. We were now way above the entrance Alicia created for us.

"Oh, that's just great," moaned Alicia.

"It's OK," said Charlotte. "We can use the boost from these spikes to bypass a few floors."

"Yes, of course!" shouted Narrisa. "Don't worry, I've got this."

She faced the uninviting black wall of Valdome Tower and opened her hands towards it, instantly, her golden beam shot out from her palms. The beam went from a dim shimmer to a bright, blinding light before it expelled from her grasp, crashing into the wall ahead.

Once the black and gold dust from the blast cleared, we could see Narrisa's efforts paid off. We now had our entrance to Valdome Tower. Swiftly, we made our way inside.

The interior of the tower was a deep purple colour, and the theme of uninviting spikes seemed to run throughout its internal structure. The corridor we found ourselves in was quiet, with no sign of any guards present. That was until we made our way around the corner.

"Stop, interlopers!" shouted an unusually high-pitched voice.

As we turned the corner, the guard who'd shouted came into view, along with a whole cluster of Huskin guards. They all vaguely resembled Zoobub, but with more impressive armour. Theirs weren't as ill-fitting as his. These Huskin guards had an evil look about them; with each of their wide eyes engulfed by its own pupils, and their fur unevenly plucked.

"Zoobub, is that you?" asked one guard in disgust. "I can't believe the rumours are true! What are you doing, leading these strange-looking things here?"

"I don't answer to you!" challenged Zoobub.

"Ha! haven't you heard? I'm the new head guard," the guard said, trying to provoke him in his squeaky voice.

"What? You! How? Why?" Zoobub replied in utter shock.

"Well, I may have used your betrayal to my benefit; expressing how I never liked you, how I knew you could never be trusted and how I should have been head guard all along," the squeaky-voiced guard openly admitted.

"You evil tantail!" Zoobub shouted, now in a complete rage.

Sophia and Ava needed to restrain him from trying to attack all the guards at once.

"Calm down, Zoobub," Ava said quietly.

"Oh, don't take it so personally, Zoobub," replied the squeaky guard. "You know how it is here; if you're not climbing over each other to reach the top, then you're scraping the bottom of the barrel. I have Huskinlings to think about. It's always been about the survival of the fittest. You know that."

"Well, it shouldn't be like that at all," stated Zoobub. "For far too long the Argonauts have treated us like slaves, making us work so hard and for what? Nothing at all!"

The guard gasped. "You shouldn't be speaking like this, Zoobub. If the Argonauts hear of your ungratefulness…"

"It doesn't matter anymore," Zoobub said, interrupting him. "I'm on the *Astro Girls'* side now, and my mission–after I help them get their friend back–is to make Huskin Valley a free place so all Huskins can live free, peaceful lives."

The squeaky-voiced guard laughed. "Have you wackered your head? That's just a silly little dream. And one you must wake up from, the sooner the better."

"Where is Metus?" I interrupted them both.

"Metus? Ha!" spat the guard. "He's far too busy to see the likes of you. Besides, you've broken several laws since you've arrived here, so you will now face the death sentence."

He put his hand into his pocket, revealing a gun.

"Death sentence? You do know who we are?" replied Sophia, amused.

Before the squeaky-voiced guard could fire his gun,

Charlotte stepped in front of him, focusing on the guard's face. From her expression, she was imagining him bellowing in uncontrollable sorrow, because that's exactly what he did.

The other guards glanced at each other, puzzled, unsure of what they should do. They had their guns out, but they were hesitating, their leader's behaviour utterly confusing them.

I immediately saw an opportunity. I remembered Korsal saying I could give inanimate objects a mind I could control. If all went well; I'd be able to exploit this confusion and take control of their weapons. Quickly, I fixed my concentration upon their guns, which started shaking in the guards' hands. Once my powers took full hold of these weapons, they ripped from the firm grips of the Huskin guards. Now, the guns were pointing right back at the guards.

"Take us to Metus," I demanded.

The guards, now our hostages, had no choice but to listen to my demand. Two of them linked their arms with the squeaky-voiced guard as his uncontrollable sobbing was only allowing him to crawl along slowly.

At the end of the corridor, we came to a stairwell. Rather dauntingly, it seemed to have endlessly twisting steps, heading down below us and up above.

"Is this the only way up?" questioned Ava.

"Wah… Yes," replied the main guard, who was still sobbing uncontrollably.

"Haven't you lot heard of elevators?" asked Narrisa.

A bubble of laughter escaped from Chloe's lips. "Ha, that was a good one."

Together we climbed the stairwell, and the whole time I tried not to think how it would take us ages to reach the top floor, especially following these little Huskin steps.

"Why did you do it, Zoobub?" one guard asked as they walked.

"Do what, Skatalls?" replied Zoobub, puzzled.

"Tricking Metus into the portal before he could get all twelve Birthstones," replied Skatalls, disappointed.

"What?" shouted Zoobub, outraged. "That is just completely talliz."

"He would say that, now that he isn't Metus's favourite Huskin anymore," the squeaky guard commented, short of breath.

Charlotte must have felt he'd sobbed enough and had therefore released him from her power. He seemed to have learnt his lesson, anyway.

"You didn't do it?" asked Skatalls, a glimmer of hope in his eyes.

"No, I didn't!" Zoobub shot back defensively. "Metus left me on Earth, and you know what? I'm glad he did."

"Oh... this isn't good, Zoobub," Skatalls told him. "Metus has branded you a traitor. He said you tricked him because you wanted to take the Birthstones for yourself."

"But it's all lies!" replied Zoobub, aghast.

"You're wanted by the Argonauts, Zoobub, dead or alive," Skatalls cried.

"Don't worry, Zoobub. No Argonauts are going to harm you. Right, girls?" I prompted.

"Right!" all the girls replied in unison.

Zoobub smiled. "Thank you," he whispered, touched.

Eventually, we could see the steps ending. Finally, we arrived at the gates to the Argonauts' lair.

METUS

Chapter 22

"Pearl and gold encrusted gates? That's a bit pretentious, isn't it?" said Narrisa.

"Ha, this is normal for the Argonauts," Zoobub explained. "They delude themselves into believing they are the highest beings on Zodiac, even higher than the Magus. Well, this is the reason the Argonauts have given themselves, anyway. But as I've said before, the real reason is because they're scared of the Empearions attacking them. So, they live up here, secluding themselves in their riches and comforts, while us

Huskins do all the hard work in truly running Argon. This place is what your civilisation would call 'luxury.'" Zoobub sighed. "Oh, why hadn't I been able to see what the Argonauts were doing to us all this time? How could I have been so talliz?"

It seemed the penny had now well and truly dropped for Zoobub.

"Can you not see what the Argonauts are doing to our kind?" Zoobub asked, turning to all the demonic-looking Huskin guards as he took his righteous stance.

"Zoobub, I think you've spent too much time with these *Astro Girls*," dismissed the squeaky-voiced guard.

"Nonsense!" Zoobub cried. "I am grateful to the *Astro Girls*, for they have opened my eyes to all this horrid exploitation at the hands of the Argonauts. And all because they're bigger, stronger, and more intimidating than us. They saw an opportunity to take advantage of our civilisation when we were first exiled from Empeariopia and they gladly took it."

At these words, all the Huskin guards argued amongst themselves.

"Enough!" shouted Skatalls after a moment. "Zoobub is right. We are all living in hardship. Some of our kind are even roaming the markets and lands, hungry, with nowhere to sleep. We work horribly long, un-Huskin hours just to put a few Nezpits on our platters. And the Argonauts? What do they do? They eat our food. They demand our workmanship…

And they work us to the ground. Some of us are even worked to death. They live in luxury while we suffer terribly. Tell me, have any of us ever seen an Argonaut experience any of the hardships we Huskins do? No, never."

The little Huskin guards looked at each other, their shoulders hunched over as the realisation set in.

I glanced at Zoobub, smiling. Hopefully, this would be the start of their revolution.

"This is all complete crab-apples," the squeaky-voiced guard said, dismissing his fellow Huskins' words.

Just then, the pearl gates slowly opened.

"Complete crab-apples?" repeated Narrisa. "Oh yes, it's so hard to see what Zoobub and Skatalls are talking about," she said sarcastically.

The reason for Narrisa's sarcasm was the sight that now lay before us, the pearl gates having opened all the way.

The sights of this hidden palace were spectacular, filled with all kinds of abundant riches as far as the eye could see. There were jewels, pearls, coins, gold, and other unknown precious metals. Even the waters ran gold here. There was no surprise to see a few little Huskins working here and there, plodding along and picking up all the wasteful leftovers from the food these Argonauts were mindlessly devouring. Luckily, they were far away from us, so they didn't notice our hostile intrusion. That, and they seemed to be in some kind of a continuous state of euphoria.

"This is the life, hey!" said Ava jokingly as we snuck past the mountain of gold to our left.

"Ah, I've been waiting for you... *Astro Girls.*"

The voice made me jump, both because the words were so unexpected and because I recognised that voice instantly. Sure enough, as we made our way around the corner, there he was: Metus.

I couldn't see any signs of Malaya, or Drayson Black. Where were they?

My heart was pounding so hard inside my chest, I breathed in deeper just to calm it. I knew I needed to keep my cool. We all needed to remain in control and let Metus know we meant business.

Unfortunately, Jasmine took that moment to cry out, "Oh Gosh, he's scary."

Metus stared at Jasmine with an unimpressed look on his face. He curled his lip up over his sharp, white pointed teeth. The surrounding treasures shimmered on his reflective scales, making him appear like some kind of golden god.

"I have been impatiently awaiting your arrival," he told us. "I was worried when I found Malaya here. She's told me so much about you all."

I wanted to scream, 'Liar!' at him then, wanted to tell him I knew exactly what happened that day because I'd been right there with Malaya. Instead, I remained silent.

"And what exactly has Malaya told you?" Elle quizzed him.

"Oh, nothing much," replied Metus. "Mostly about how lovely and kind you all are."

This 'caring character' he was faking was so obvious, it sickened me; anyone would have seen right through it.

"Ahem, did you forget something on your travels?" hinted Zoobub.

Metus fiercely glared at Zoobub for a split second before shouting, "Oh, Zoobub! Where have you been? I thought I'd lost you!" He bowed his head as he wiped a non-existent tear from his eye.

In response, Zoobub shook his head in disappointment.

"*Astro Girls*, there is no need for this hostile approach," said Metus. "We're all friends here. You can let my precious Huskins go now; I'll take you to Malaya. I know you must be missing her dearly."

"No!" shouted Ava as the guards started to leave. "We'll hang onto them if it's all the same to you."

"Yes, of course," Metus begrudgingly replied, sighing.

Keeping a lookout as we went, we followed Metus deeper into this golden palace, passing by several golden pillars until we reached a solitary chamber.

"I will wait here and let you all have a private

moment with Malaya," said Metus. "It's the least I can do."

"You two, open the door!" ordered Narrisa, pointing at the first two Huskin guards.

The guards quietly went forth as Narrisa instructed and opened the doors to the chamber.

The inside was so dark; it was hard to see anything.

"It's too dark in there," said Amelia, turning to face Metus.

"Ah, why yes," replied the Argonaut. "Sorry about that. There must be something wrong with the lighting."

Somehow, without him even moving a muscle, the overly waxed candles on the walls lit themselves, showing the internal structure of the chamber. It was surprisingly large; it just went on and on.

We edged in with the utmost caution, knowing it was a trap but also knowing Malaya must be here somewhere. After coming so far, we were just moments from saving her.

I wondered if she was still trapped inside that cage Ethereal showed us, but somehow, I doubted it. Going by Metus's act, he'd probably had her all scrubbed up, as though she'd always been well looked after.

The igniting flare of the candles weakened to a stable burn, and as we squinted into the distance, an opulent glow teased us. We trekked closer towards it until it was in full view.

There she was.

My stomach twisted. Oh, Malaya. Poor Malaya.

After the immediate rush of relief at seeing her wore off, I paid more attention to Malaya's situation. She was floating unresponsively in some kind of nebula, her appearance unchanged from the last moment we were together.

Oh no, was she still breathing? Was she even still alive?

"You! What's wrong with her?" I raged, demanding an answer from the squeaky-voiced Huskin guard.

"I... I... don't know..." he replied, panicking and then running out of the chamber with his guards right behind him.

"But I do," announced a mysterious voice, lurking in the gloom.

When he stepped out of the darkness, a shock jolted through my body. To see him like that... with a dark kind of mischief in his eyes, standing beside Malaya with absolutely no sympathy on his features. To see how he was controlling her via his Huskin-made arm wodge... It made my stomach churn to see what had become of Drayson Black.

TREACHERY

Chapter 23

"Mr Black? Why?" cried Ava.

"Why? Why what?" he asked. "Why have I decided to align myself with a much greater civilisation than the one I come from? A civilisation which just so happens to be millions of light years ahead of pathetic Earth? And not just in a physical sense, but a technological one too? I can become anything here. I can be far greater than I was ever allowed to be on Earth. Humans only ever made fun of me... questioning my genius... questioning all my long years of research and making a mockery of me all over the world. If they could see me now, they'd think twice before laughing at me," he announced.

"What have you done to Malaya?" demanded Elle, ignoring his self-righteous statement.

"Ah, Malaya, she is now in an unconscious state. You see, with all this brilliant Huskin technology I was able to make something truly magnificent. Something into which I could immerse my own genius mind to create a tool that could diffuse the vessels the Birthstones inhabit. Now, this wasn't easy. No. You see, the Birthstones immediately make the bearers a different class of 'being' altogether. Think of it as more of an ultimate upgrade than one could ever hope to ask for. So, as you can imagine, I am delighted to see my efforts in disabling the vessel whilst also keeping the Birthstone unharmed have worked beautifully," he gloated coldly.

"Unconscious state? Diffuse the vessel?" I asked, shaking my head. "Look! I don't know what you're trying to accomplish here, or what lies Metus has told you to make you do this, but I do know he's only interested in getting all the Birthstones for himself. His history can tell you that. I mean, look at how the Argonauts have treated the Huskin race, and how they ambushed the Empearions, killing all their heirs."

"Ha! Don't you worry your little head about matters that don't concern you," Drayson said dismissively before raising his arm. "I have my collateral, I will be alongside Metus, as his equal. So please, do not question alliances you don't fully understand."

"You're a fool!" shouted Chloe. "Do you really think he'll 'lower' himself enough to have a human by his side? He used you. He captured Malaya so he could get all twelve Birthstones here. And now he's going to kill us all..." She trailed off, her voice failing her.

"Please, Drayson," pleaded Amelia, "you have to see it isn't just us you're endangering. This is bigger than all of us."

"Ha!" Drayson spat. "Very convincing, girls. Did your devious Huskin friend put you up to this? No matter, I know how to deal with you all."

"Oh! It's nice to see you don't have any hatred towards us Huskins," Zoobub said sarcastically, before jumping to the floor and placing his hands over his head, cowering.

Drayson smirked as he raised his bulky arm wodge towards Malaya. "Now, I am going to press this big button, like so, and if you carefully watch your friend, you will see fragments starting to lift around her Birthstone. The purpose of this is to carefully remove the precious stone from the vessel. Now, I must stress the utmost care will be taken to only keep the stone intact, which will override any attention to care for the vessel it inhabits. I guess what I'm trying to say is only one element in this separation will be safe, while the other... well..." He shrugged casually.

"Will die," Narrisa finished, her voice no louder than a whisper.

"No! Please stop!" bellowed Alicia.

"I can't believe you're doing this!" raged Chloe. "I can't believe a so-called genius like yourself can't see how reckless you're being right now."

"Oh really? So now you little girls all think you're so wise and knowledgeable because you have a few rocks in your chests? Well, we'll see how clever you all are once you've joined your lifeless friend," Drayson sneered.

With that, he swiftly pointed the arm wodge toward us, and in the same instance we completely fanned out, Zoe being the fastest off the mark to counter a defence. She used her ability to create duplicate illusions of us all so Drayson wouldn't know which of us were the real *Astro Girls*.

As expected, Drayson seemed amazed to witness first-hand the capability of our powers at play. After a moment, however, he shook himself from his wide-eyed reaction; pressing down confidently amongst the countless buttons on the top panel of his arm wodge.

The risk was clear. I just hoped he wouldn't get lucky on the first attempt and capture all of us hidden amongst the illusion, resigning us to the same fate as Malaya.

Drayson started pointing his arm wodge back

and forth as he contemplated exactly where he should release his fire. He was trying to find a glitch or a fault in the illusion Zoe created, any little sign that would expose the original *Astro Girls*.

He shrugged when he could find none, before lifting his hold on the button, causing fire to expel from the arm wodge with fine-tuned precision. It effortlessly burnt through the first three illusions, one at a time.

"Ahh!" cried Zoe. "It's so weird. I can feel the attack inside my mind."

It was clear she was struggling to keep the power of her illusions up.

"Someone else has to take over. I can't hold it much longer!" she shouted.

Immediately we all felt the tremendous pressure of trying to think of something on the spot that would be as great as Zoe's defence, but we pondered for too long. The quick-witted Drayson took his chance.

He tapped again at his arm wodge, releasing a gusting force so powerful he needed to hold up his arm with the other.

It seemed as though the force was feeding off itself, violently rotating until it funnelled into a wind-thrashing tornado. There was no escaping from its immediate growing hunger, which inevitably engulfed us all.

We were whirling around powerlessly, unable

to regain a single ounce of control as we bashed and bumped into one another. It felt as if we were dried up and weightless; like autumn leaves caught inside a violent windstorm.

As I fought against the force, a voice spoke out inside the stillest depths of my mind.

"Girls, I have an idea. When you next collide with someone, use its impact to push each other as far away as possible."

It was Sophia, using her telepathic ability to communicate her tactic.

I briefly imagined how I could implement what Sophia suggested. The motion inside this tornado was tremendously unstable, and we didn't have any control whatsoever. I mean, what if, on the next collision, my back slammed straight into someone else's? I couldn't use that collision to propel myself as far away as possible. After a bit more thought, I concluded using a pair of limbs to act as a spring would be ideal, though this wouldn't be an easy task.

Glancing straight ahead, I focused intently to see which of my friends I was most likely to collide with next.

Amelia seemed to be the next one being forced in my direction by the high winds, and we locked eyes as the fate of our collision became increasingly certain. With great effort, we tried to continue facing each other so we could use the impact to our full advantage.

My hands were aiming for Amelia's shoulders; I could see she'd already chosen to use the opposing limbs by the way she'd brought her knees towards her chest, exposing the soles of her feet towards me.

Her petite sized three feet connected with my mid thighs, but I didn't look down at them; instead, I kept eye contact with Amelia. My hands simultaneously locked onto her shoulders, and we concurrently bent our limbs, bringing our bodies close together, ready for dramatically springing back in the opposite direction.

We both nodded in sync. Three... two... one. As we released our coiled limbs into springing action, I stretched and straightened with the predominant thought of propelling myself as far away as I could. My emerald green colour was flowing around my entire body as this thought grew stronger. It was my aura visibly showing; I'd ignited my flying ability. In utter excitement, I glanced around, and just as I found my flying abilities, so too did the rest of the *Astro Girls*. We were all hovering inside the whirlwind, with full control of our bodies and the widest grins on our faces.

Narrisa, Jasmine, and Charlotte looked at one another and began flying in the opposite direction to the whirlwind. They spun faster and faster until they matched the speed of the opposing winds, this action continuing to weaken the gust until it vanished. Together, the three of them used their mutual air element to disable Drayson's synthetic wodge-made air attack.

Drayson was now raging, and he immediately made another attempt to restrain us. He gave a final tap on his arm wodge, releasing an overshadowing speckle of glittered darkness, the same kind of nebula which encased Malaya. The deadly outer radius of this nebula was so powerful and deeply rooted, it immediately took hold of all eleven of us.

It was completely unexpected. The glittery dance the nebula gave us had been a distraction so it could work quickly behind the scenes and trap us by paralysis.

There was no denying we'd put up a great defence, but Drayson had finally captured us.

It was a torturous situation to be in, completely frozen, unable to move. My mind continued as normal, amplifying all my emotions—regret, unfairness, anger, sadness, injustice, confusion, and the terrifying realisation of what was about to take place.

The nebula encased our bodies, shifting us from mid-air to just above the floor. Our heads were placed beside one another, and with our toes facing outward, he'd arranged us to form a perfect circle.

My position within this circle gave me the perfect view of Drayson. He was smiling in a self-congratulatory way, happy to see us captured, to see us under his full control. "Zoobub, come out of your cowering crouch and witness how 'unbeatable' your new friends are now!" he shouted, adding a sardonic laugh.

Zoobub had been cowering on the floor this whole time, and now as he looked up, he started shaking. Drayson sneered at Zoobub as though he were pathetic and grabbed him by the scruff of the neck, forcing him to stare at us. For a moment, I didn't think it would be possible for his eyes to look even bigger than they naturally were. Glazed over in complete fear and sorrow, it was obvious he was holding back his tears with a huge, grave effort. Slowly, he shook his head, unable to speak.

FRIEND OR FOE

Chapter 24

A slow clapping sound echoed around the chamber as Metus came into view behind Drayson.

"Well done, my compeer. I never doubted you for a second," gloated Metus.

"Th-hank you. See, I told you they were nothing more than juveniles," Drayson replied in utter relief as he released Zoobub's neck.

"Yes. Ah, I see you have already started extracting the Birthstone from this one," Metus said as he walked past Malaya, looking over her unconscious form. "Oh, this excites me very much. But why have we not started extracting the stones from the others?" he asked, his impatience strengthening.

"I-I understand your eagerness to have all the stones right now, but I'm afraid to say the others will have to go through the exact same process as the first one went through. S-so that the Birthstones have the best chance of remaining unharmed," explained Drayson.

"Are you telling me I have to wait even longer?" Metus questioned sternly.

Drayson nervously cleared his throat. "I-if I rush the process, th-then it could destroy the Birthstones and our entire existence," stuttered Drayson, his voice quivering.

"I dislike waiting. In fact, the sheer thought of having to wait just one minute longer makes me very, *very* angry! I want all the Birthstones now! And if I don't get them now, well, let's just say that my fellow Argonauts can finally see what you taste like," Metus threatened Drayson.

"What?" shouted Drayson, alarmed. "B-but y-you need me. I'm the only one who knows how to extract these Birthstones. You can't just kill me off. You need me!" he blurted out. "What about our agreement?"

"You stupid Earth people!" Metus shouted, almost laughing. "Honestly, what's wrong with your kind? Why do you all think, for some reason unknown to the cosmic web, that you all have a divine right to be a part of the magnificent force these Birthstones bring? It baffles me, it really does." He shook his head in disbelief.

"Metus," said Zoobub, "if I may interject—"

Metus turned aggressively toward Zoobub as though angered this Huskin called him by name.

Zoobub looked nervously to the ground, rubbing the bottom of his toes back and forth against the gold-plated floor. He said, "If the Magus Priest bestowed the Birthstones to the *Astro Girls*, then maybe this should be respected by all beings."

"Ha! Well, well, look what we have here!" Metus shouted. "The runt traitor Zoobub finally grows a backbone! Well, clearly the Magus Priests have all gone looney in their old age. It's time for a new era to arise. It's time for the Argonauts to rule the *entire* cosmic web," Metus added proudly, holding his head up whilst he envisioned his great plan.

"Yes, you're right, the looney-ness has definitely become an issue here," Zoobub remarked out loud without thinking. When he realised what he'd said, he squealed in fright and threw his hands over his mouth.

"How dare you! First you have the nerve to call me by my name and then you mock me? You? Of all beings!" Metus shouted in a furious rage, stretching his entire arm backwards and then swinging it forwards, hitting Zoobub with brutal force.

WHACK!

Zoobub flew up into the air, and as quickly as he'd smacked into the ridiculously high ceiling, he plummeted straight back down onto the cold, hard-plated ground. Then Zoobub lay there, flopped to one side, as though the blow sent him into the deepest sleep.

Horror clutched at my heart to see him gasping for breath before he became utterly, terribly still.

I was heartbroken. I couldn't believe I'd been forced to watch this horror unfold, unable to protect this sweet little creature who'd become one of our dearest friends. I was raging with anger to see Zoobub's life taken so ruthlessly, to be ripped so coldly from his teacup-sized grasp. Tears welled in my eyes, blurring my vision, and to make matters worse, I couldn't blink them clear. In that moment, I felt like I was trapped in a coffin, buried alive and unable to escape. I was screaming, shouting, and uncontrollably blubbering, but it was all for nothing. All my feelings and emotions couldn't be physically released while I was still in this paralysed state. I couldn't even twitch.

At this realisation I tried to calm myself down. I couldn't fall into the trap of getting all worked up and losing all hope, which would inevitably lead to our deaths. If that were to happen, Zoobub would have died for nothing. So instead, I reached out and called for Sophia, sure her telepathic ability would still be functioning.

"Sophia! Can you hear me?" I shouted within my mind.

"Yes," came her reply. "I can't believe Drayson caught us, but don't worry; Alicia is working on a plan. I heard Zoobub talking to Metus. What happened? Can you see anything?"

"I saw everything. Zoobub is dead!" I cried. "Metus just killed him! We have to break free and stop him."

"What do you mean, he's dead? He can't be! Oh, this is horrible. Poor Zoobub," replied a Sophia, her words filled with grief.

"Look, what can we do to get out?" I asked, trying to ignite an idea–any idea.

"Alicia's already working on sabotaging Drayson's arm wodge with her electronic ability. She said it's really difficult because of the Huskin craftsmanship, but she's nearly broken through."

"Let's hope she manages to break through before it's too late," I said.

Leaving Zoobub on the floor, Metus walked over to Drayson. "I believe I've just demonstrated how those who act against me are likely to end up," Metus said ominously.

"Y-yes, yes. Please. Let me see what I can do," pleaded Drayson, stroking his precious arm wodge. However, as soon as Metus turned his back on him, Drayson gave him a sharp, revengeful stare before shouting, "But you're forgetting, you don't have the Birthstones yet."

With that, Drayson pointed his arm wodge at Metus and, further proclaiming his vengeance, he then pressed down hard on the panel of the arm wodge, which shuddered and shook uncontrollably. And then, a second later...

BOOM!

The entire arm wodge exploded, its blast throwing Metus and Drayson in opposite directions and knocking them both out cold.

I couldn't help but smile. Alicia's effort worked.

The surrounding nebula vanished, and we dropped to the floor. Now the arm wodge was no longer an active threat, we were free from its gripping paralysis.

"Yes! You did it, Alicia!" Sophia shouted, delighted.

"Wow, I did, didn't I?" replied Alicia as the realisation sunk in.

"Malaya!" I exclaimed, looking over at her. Alicia's plan to break the arm wodge had also freed Malaya. She was sitting on the floor, looking around and blinking, utterly confused.

We all ran over to her, giving her a long and overdue hug.

"Phew, we really thought we'd lost you for a moment," Ava said, her voice full of relief.

"Argh, my head!" Malaya cried, putting her hand up to her left temple. After blinking a few more times, she looked at her friends and smiled. "Wow, my head must need longer to come around, you all look so different. I can't believe you all risked your lives to come and save me. I love you guys so much. Thank you."

"I've been feeling so guilty," I admitted, "especially as I was there when Metus took you." I reached out and squeezed her hand. "What happened after that?"

"What? You shouldn't feel guilty at all," Malaya said. "It wasn't your fault, and I haven't blamed you for a second." She smiled before continuing, "Metus had me caged up straight away. He managed to turn Drayson against us by telling him he could rule the universe alongside Metus, but only if he could get the stones from us. So, Drayson found a way to tweak the Huskin arm wodge thing and then he tested it out on an innocent homeless Huskin, right in front of me." She shuddered. "When he was satisfied with the result, he used it on me. That's all I remember."

"Well, they're both out cold now," remarked Jasmine.

"And it serves them right," added Narrisa.

The rest of us nodded in agreement.

"Malaya, did you know you always had your powers? You were the one who opened the portal" Ava revealed.

"I only realised when Sophia contacted me to open it up again so you all could come and save me. By the way, I like your new look."

Malaya complimented us, looking us up and down.

"Oh yes, that reminds me," said Chloe. "The Magus Priest told us to give you this."

Chloe handed Malaya the tiny red embossed box.

"What do I do with it?" asked Malaya, puzzled.

"Er, they didn't tell me that part. Open it, I guess?" suggested Chloe.

Without hesitation, Malaya opened the box, and as she lifted its lid, the box floated out of her hand, garnet red rays streaming from within it. Korsal's chant echoed around Malaya and we stood back, knowing she was about to experience the *Astro Girl* transformation.

Once the gust disappeared, Malaya finally had her green and brown themed outfit, her eyes and hair now an intense garnet red.

"Oh wow, this is amazing!" she announced.

"It suits you," I said, smiling, though the smile dropped off my face the instant I thought of Zoobub. I looked towards where his body rested and broke away from the reuniting huddle of girls to be with poor, sweet Zoobub. Saddened, the girls followed my lead.

COME TO BLOWS

Chapter 25

I collapsed beside Zoobub, and once I'd confirmed he'd stopped breathing, I started sobbing uncontrollably as I rested my forehead on his still, miniature potbelly. "We didn't even get to tell you about the Magus Priests' home," I cried.

"Let me try and heal him," urged Narrisa.

Narrisa kneeled down in front of Zoobub, on the opposite side to me, and hovered both her hands over his body. When she closed her eyes to focus, Narrisa's unmistakable golden beam of light shone from both her palms.

Quietly, I wiped the tears from my eyes, getting a better view while I desperately clung onto some kind of hope.

She started from the centre of his body, moving her hands in opposite directions until her right hand was hovering over his head and her left over his feet. She then returned her hands to their central starting position and the golden beam ceased. We waited for a few moments, examining every inch of his body for any sign of movement, but it was all for nothing. Narrisa's efforts seemed to have no effect. Zoobub was still lying there, utterly lifeless.

"I'm so sorry, Zoobub," whispered Narrisa as she opened her eyes, saddened she couldn't save him.

"Please… no! Oh, why didn't it work?" cried Ava.

"I don't know. Maybe I can't bring anyone back from the dead," guessed Narrisa.

"This Huskin is important?" Malaya asked the rest of us. "How did you guys know him?"

"Do you remember that little Huskin who came out of the portal after Metus?" I reminded her.

"No… yes. It was him? But he was the one who told Metus we were hiding in the trees. If he'd never said that, I wouldn't have been taken," complained Malaya.

"That's true," I replied, "but there's more to it than that. Up until shortly after that moment, Zoobub was made to believe he was Metus's 'trusted guard', but Metus purposely left him on Earth. Zoobub soon came to realise Metus was nothing more than a selfish liar. He helped us find our way through Zodiac to come and save you. He became a dear friend to all of us. We couldn't have made it here without him, we owe him our lives," I explained with a quivering voice before bursting out into tears.

"I understand now," Malaya replied, empathising with our loss.

"I guess we should all go back home now we have Malaya," suggested Charlotte. "Our parents must be worried."

"Not so fast!" a chilling voice announced from behind us.

Startled, we all jumped and turned towards the voice. It was Metus.

"After all, you have something that belongs to me," Metus added, readying himself to fight us.

"Malaya, can you teleport Zoobub back to his home?" I asked, wanting to keep his body out of harm's way.

"When will you get it through your head? These stones are not yours!" yelled Chloe.

"Look, I'll be nice about it. Give me the Birthstones now and I'll let you go home. You can all pretend none of this happened and go back to your pathetic little lives," Metus sneered.

"Why should we listen to you?" asked Sophia. "We already have the Birthstones, and their powers."

"I tried to be nice, but reasoning with you *Astro Girls* won't work. I was hoping we could end this amicably, but I guess I'll just have to rip the stones out of your stubborn chests myself. You see, a serpent's venom can kill or cure. I choose to kill," he ended in a threatening tone.

With that, Metus charged towards us.

Malaya worked fast, teleporting Zoobub's body safely out of this chamber. As Metus drew closer, he sped up even faster, and Elle generated her force push, blasting it straight at him. Metus flew backwards, breaking his charge. The force attack Elle used only seemed to temporarily deflect his intention to harm us, however, as once again he regained control and rampaged towards us. This time, Jasmine fired her laser attack, but the rays from her laser weren't affecting him; they just bounced off his scaly skin. His ability to deflect our attacks stunned us, but that didn't mean we'd give up.

Seeing that Jasmine's laser attack wasn't working, I tried my body control ability to stop Metus right in his tracks. I focused hard, trying to stop him, but he wasn't even slowing down. It was as though my powers were useless against him. I felt a horrid, heavy feeling overwhelm me. Maybe we'd completely missed something here.

"My powers aren't working on him!" I shouted in frustration.

"Neither is my emotion manipulation!" added Charlotte.

"Nor my illusion attacks!" seconded Zoe.

Metus laughed.

We now realised Metus could deflect mind attacks and even physical attacks, seeing as it only bought us a few seconds before he resumed his charge again. In fact, Metus was getting closer and closer, seemingly unscathed by our previous attempts to stop him.

Narrisa tried to cast a deflective spell to at least slow Metus down, but yet again, it didn't work.

Then, as Metus reached us once more to attack, Chloe used her shapeshifting powers to morph into Metus, jumping in his way.

"*Yes! Go on, Chloe!*" I shouted, me and the rest of the girls cheering her on.

Chloe was now at equal physical strength to Metus, and because of this, she could use Metus's brute force against him. They both rammed, kicked, pushed, and threw each other around. They were a complete match, the only differences being their own unique minds and Chloe's visible agate Birthstone now embedded in her scaly skin.

Metus knew what to do; he aimed for Chloe's embedded Birthstone. He threw her down to the ground, pressing his foot heavily upon her diaphragm.

Chloe struggled to break free as Metus fixed his creepy long fingers around her yellow agate Birthstone.

"Oh no!" shouted Charlotte.

"Malaya! Quickly!" shouted Elle as she readied herself to strike. Elle then shot her power at Metus, forcing him away from Chloe. And, having prompted Malaya in time, she too lined her power up to open a portal next to them. Chloe quickly forced Metus into the portal, which Malaya immediately shut behind him.

"Argh! Good riddance!" Narrisa shouted, exhausted but relieved.

"Ditto! Thanks for the help," agreed Chloe.

"Where did you send him, Malaya?" asked Jasmine.

"I'm not sure, I just thought of a place that has nothing… like an empty part of space, far away from any being he could hurt or manipulate ever again."

"Did anyone see what happened to Drayson?" asked Ava, looking around us, puzzled.

"He was lying over there, but now he's gone," Alicia said, frowning.

"Great, that's a loose end I bet we'll regret not tying up," sighed Elle.

Before anyone could say anything else, the most bizarre sound reached our ears; the sound of trumpets. It was as if someone, somewhere, was playing a fanfare.

We made our way out of the chamber and back on

the palace grounds, all the Argonauts seemed to have been fleeing.

We soon saw who was coming.

An array of slender-framed beings marched up towards us in the long chamber. They all had beautifully long iridescent hair, high prominent cheekbones, bushy-shaped eyebrows, and shimmering skin. They formed into two lines, three of them standing on either side, facing each other with the greatest posture, as they continued to blow their trumpets. Then, two well-groomed beings appeared between the rows, walking elegantly towards us. One was holding a scroll and the other a cloudy crystal ball.

"Ahem." One being, the apparent messenger, cleared it's throat before announcing, "*Astro Girls*, Tunker Eric and Tunket Josephine of Empeariopia request the pleasure of your company."

Then, as soon as they'd arrived, they left again.

"Should we follow them?" Narrisa asked, confused.

"Yeah, and we'd better be quick!" replied Zoe, running behind them.

We all shrugged and rushed to follow.

EMPEARIOPIA

Chapter 26

We followed the messengers for what felt like miles, through several hidden tunnel systems that finally led us all outside. Initially, we were overwhelmed by the immediate rush of bright light shining on our faces. After adjusting to it, we could see we were now standing on white mountains, their tips covered in pale-green snow. As I looked out, I took in the striking views of Empeariopia. It was breathtaking.

The skies here were a luscious green, as were the lakes and the sea. The woodland areas scattered across were heavy in different hues of blue, and in between there were clusters of elegant, high white buildings. Above me, the clouds were pale yellow, the soil beneath my feet, white.

We travelled down the mountains, through the ancient forests; home to many alien-looking, majestic creatures. Taking in all these peculiar sights spurred a sad thought- I wish Zoobub was here, I bet he would have loved to have seen all of this.

Finally, we reached what must have been the Kingdom Castle of Empeariopia. Its architecture stretched tall; its bricks made from what appeared to be unspoilt white marble, its windows covered in grand arches. There was a Norse Viking feel to the place. The buildings were married to nature, both intertwining; it was tranquil and utterly serene.

"It is a pleasure to finally meet you all, *Astro Girls*," welcomed Tunker Eric, who approached us from the entrance of the building, his arms wide open in a welcoming gesture.

"Thank you for inviting us," said Elle politely.

"You have a truly beautiful kingdom here," added Jasmine, in awe of the whole place.

"Thank you," said Tunket Josephine, smiling. "We heard the great news of your defeat of the Argonaut, Metus. You have all done a great service to the cosmic web."

"Really, that quick? Wow, news travels fast here in

Zodiac," stated Charlotte, impressed.

"We have eyes and ears everywhere," replied Tunker Eric.

"We are glad it's finally over. It was difficult to defeat Metus," I admitted, puzzled. "It was as if he was able to deflect most of our powers somehow."

"Really? Oh, then, maybe the great myths are true," pondered Tunket Josephine, a worried expression clouded her beautifully structured face. "I regret to say, he must be holding Ophiuchus.

"What is Ophiuchus?" questioned Malaya, puzzled.

"The myths state it's the thirteenth star sign, the 'serpent bearer," remarked Tunker Eric.

"Wait a minute! Thirteenth star sign? I thought there were only twelve!" exclaimed Narrisa.

"Yes, it seems we have all regrettably made this very same mistake, but it is the only logical way he could have shielded from your powers," Tunket Josephine explained. "According to the myth of the constellations, Ophiuchus was cast out of the cosmos, never really given a place amongst the twelve star signs, the reason for this decision was never made known. But if my suspicion is correct then Metus, somehow has Ophiuchus and knows of its unheard secrets. If this is true, there is no doubt he will come for you all again."

"But Malaya sent him far away, safely away from

any being," reassured Jasmine.

"How sure can you be? He found his way to you before, had he not?" challenged Tunker Eric. Tunket Josephine rested her slender hand on his shoulder.

"Now, you all successfully stopped Metus this time, but please make no mistake. Until he is slayed, and that black scapolite stone is removed from his wicked corpse, nowhere in the cosmic web will be safe from his evil."

"I believe you," I replied. "We've all seen just how wicked Metus is, he ended the life of a dear friend of ours." I bowed my head sadly.

"Oh, you mean Zoobub?" asked Tunket Josephine excitedly.

"Yes… sorry?" I replied, raising my head at her inappropriately placed excitement.

"Yes! Zoobub, he is here," continued Tunket Josephine.

"What do you mean, he's here?" I questioned, feeling utterly puzzled as I looked to Malaya.

"Hey, I didn't know where his home was," she said, shrugging.

"So, you sent him to the Empearions?" I asked, baffled.

Just then Zoobub came running out of the building towards us, and upon seeing him alive and well, we all rushed over to him, utterly delighted.

"Zoobub! How?" asked Narrisa, putting her hands

over her mouth in shock.

"You saved me, Narrisa, you brought me back," Zoobub replied, hugging Narrisa's leg.

"But we waited... It didn't work!" Narrisa responded, confused.

"No, it definitely did!" Zoobub replied, looking down at his body pointedly. "You *Astro Girls* are just too impatient."

"Oh, Zoobub! It's amazing to have you back. And you look so much better without all that armour on. You even look a little taller!" I said, joyful tears welling in my eyes as I leaned down to pat his furry head.

"So, what will you all do now?" questioned Tunker Eric.

"Go back to Earth," answered Amelia. "Our families must be worried."

"But what about Metus? You only sent him away... He'll come back for you all," warned Tunket Josephine.

"Yes, he will, and we'll all be ready for him when he does," responded Malaya confidently.

We all nodded in agreement.

After we'd all said goodbye to the Tunker and Tunket, Malaya reached her arms out to open a portal back home. We were all so excited to finally go back; it felt like it had been forever since I'd seen my family. I looked back at Zoobub. "Are you coming?" I questioned.

Just as we all stepped into the portal home, Zoobub shrugged and followed.

Moments later we arrived back where it all began, inside the clearing. It looked exactly how we'd left it, and Ethereal was there, ready to welcome our safe return.

"*Astro Girls*, look at you! It's as if the Birthstones were made for you all along. You have all come into your roles proudly, and you have grown into the perfect alliance."

She smiled, looking at us each in turn as she spoke.

"You all had your own demons to face, which you overcame in order to strengthen your self-worth… That is a powerful base to build upon. It will be exciting to see what adventures the future will hold for you all, and I will continue to guide you through it, though only when you truly need it."

"Thank you, Ethereal, for watching over us," Amelia said gratefully.

"Yes, thanks," said Narrisa, before adding, "but I have to say, there were times when I felt we could have used your guidance and you didn't show up."

"Ah, you must understand that giving guidance is an art," Ethereal explained. "If too much is given, then your journey would be controlled by another, and you should never let anyone hold that power."

"Wow, that was deep, and it actually made sense," replied Narrisa, pleasantly surprised. The rest of us nodded in agreement.

"Ethereal, is the thirteenth Birthstone true? Does Metus really possess it?" asked Chloe, frowning.

"Yes, Tunker Eric and Tunket Josephine's suspicions are correct. He is Ophiuchus, the serpent bearer, and he holds the black scapolite stone," Ethereal said, sounding even more serious now. "He will be back, and you must all be ready to defeat him once and for all when he does. The future of the cosmic web will be relying on your success."

"Great," groaned Charlotte, "I was hoping this was all over."

"Not quite just yet. *Astro Girls*, I will be seeing you again soon," Ethereal assured us before vanishing once again.

"I can't believe we actually did it! We made it back home, with Malaya and all in one piece!" announced Elle.

As the gratefulness to this reality sunk in, we all smiled and nodded in agreement, me taking this time to squeeze on Zoobub's cheek.

"Ah, home sweet home! So, now we're back what do we do?" questioned Jasmine.

"I guess we continue with our normal Earth lives until we're needed again?" said Zoe, shrugging.

"I bet that'll be sooner than I'd hope," remarked Narrisa.

We all agreed, and as we all wanted to rush home

and see our families, we decided to catch up on the group chat later. Though we gave each other a big group hug before we temporally went our separate ways.

As I walked, I was readying myself to explain why I'd taken so long, why I looked so different, and why I had a Huskin… pet?… with me. Oh, this part would be hard, never mind the world-changing events we'd just experienced, saving the entire cosmic web. I chuckled as I edged closer to the front door. Then, taking a deep breath, I walked in.

"Mum, I'm back. Sorry I'm so late," I apologised, not even looking at the clock.

"You're back early!" Mum shouted from the kitchen. "Did you forget something?"

Confused, I paused and reversed my step to peer at the digital clock in the hall. It was only a few hours after I'd left, and it was the same date too!

Amazed, I walked into the kitchen, great butterflies appearing in my stomach as Mum looked me over, then her gaze dropped to where Zoobub stood.

"Since when do we have a dog, Arianna?"

Wait! What? Why did she think Zoobub was a dog? And why wasn't she upset about my new look? It made no sense.

Zoobub looked at me and shrugged.

"Maybe it's Zoe, using her illusion abilities again," he said. Then added, "What's a dog?"

"He's cute," Mum said, "but I hope he's not going to bark like that all the time."

It made sense then. We would need a disguise, back here I mean. No going back to school with freakishly, vibrant-coloured hair and eyes now. We'd stand out like sore thumbs. We'd also have a lot of explaining to do. Things no one on Earth would ever understand. We had to hide in plain sight until Metus made his next move.

I motioned to Zoobub to keep quiet and then stared at my mum, relieved she was oblivious to my new life.

"Mum, can we keep him? Please? I promise I'll take good care of him and everything," I pleaded.

"Well, I'll check with Brad, but I don't see why not? Why don't you take him outside? Dinner's not ready for a while yet."

"Thanks, Mum. You're the best." I gave her the biggest hug. "Wait here," I told Zoobub. "I'll be right back."

I raced to my room to grab my laptop. After all, I had a lot of writing to do.

About the author

 **ISHA PANESAR** is the debut author of Astro Girls — celestial bond, the first novel in its intended trilogy. Isha was born and raised by her widowed mother and older sister in Heston, Middlesex. In her childhood, Isha was always getting into mischief along with her little brother (Such things like pouring her mum's expensive perfume down the sink!).

In school, Isha struggled to pay attention and would often find herself caught in a daydream. She was bottom set in every class and her only salvageable grade directed her toward fashion as she entered college.

English was never her strongest subject but daydreaming and the world of fantasy was. It's where she stumbled across the idea for Astro Girls, built around all mystical things that she loves — astrology, superpowers, fantasy worlds, space, aliens as well as good triumphing over evil, moral values, believing in your abilities and finding your inner strength.

Isha has always believed from her heart that anything you put your mind to you will succeed, it was this very belief which kept her going in completing this novel. No matter how tired she was whilst working those 10-hour shifts and raising her two beautiful children. Today, Isha proudly voices her novel Astro Girls is female-driven, aimed to inspire and ignite the greatness in all who read it.

Isha lives in Surrey, UK. Sharing her life with her loving fiancé a nd t heir t wo c hildren. W hen s he's n ot dreaming of Astro Girls and the empowering greatness behind it, she can be found elbow-deep in pizza dough — she loves cooking!

If you wish to know when Isha's next book will come out, please visit her website at

www.astrogirlsofficial.com

where you can subscribe for the latest news and visit her social media links.